Saving West

Tennessee U Series, Book 1

Denver Shaw

Denver Shaw Romance

This is a work of fiction. All characters, places, businesses, and incidents are from the author's imagination or they are used fictitiously and are definitely fictionalized. Any trademarks or pictures herein are not authorized by the trademark owners and do not in any way mean the work is sponsored by or associated with the trademark owners. Any trademarks or pictures used are specifically in a descriptive capacity. Any resemblance to actual events, locales, or persons living or dead, is coincidental.

Contents

Blurb

How far would you go to save someone?

I can't afford any distractions. I've been put on academic probation and I'm one mistake away from being expelled and losing everything I've worked so hard for. All I want is to make my mother proud and honor her memory by getting my degree. My plan this semester is to keep my head down, focus on my studies, and stay out of trouble.

But fate is fickle and it seems like she has other plans when she suddenly dumps *him* at my feet. Weston Perkins, the university's star football player.

He's the worst kind of distraction — beautiful and vicious, arrogant and hot as sin, troubled and vulnerable.

I can't bear to be around him, and yet, I can't seem to stay away. But the more time I spend with him, the more I realize that there is something very wrong with West.

He's harboring a dark secret and desperately needs a friend.

I'm going to help West, even if he doesn't want it, and even if it means putting my future on the line.

Because some things in life are worth getting in trouble for.

Saving West is a slow-burn, emotional, hurt/comfort MM romance with moderate angst and a hard-earned HEA

Chapter 1

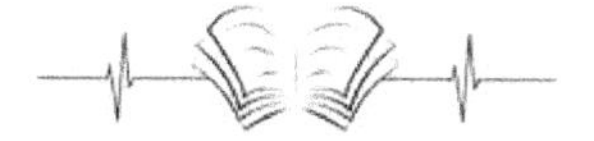

Shane

One more mistake and you're out of Tennessee University.

The words echo in my head as I walk through campus, the fall air crisp and cool against my skin. I run a hand through my hair, trying to clear my mind. The warning is clear. One toe out of line, one word too many, and my time here is over. My future would be ruined.

I have until the end of the semester to turn my life around, according to the disciplinary committee that allowed me to attend TU. Although, I suspect that my uncle being the dean of the university had more to do with my admittance than their belief in my ability to change.

As if I did something wrong in the first place.

I stop for a moment at a fork in one of the paths leading around campus. Going right leads back to my dorm. Going left leads into the dark corners of campus. The ones that are perfect for trying to take my mind off the mess that is my life.

If I were still in high school, I would turn left without hesitation. I would head to the party I heard was being thrown. Old me would laugh, drink, and dance, looking for a cute guy to hook up with and forget all my problems. The old Shane wouldn't have a care in the world. He would party until all of his problems were in the past and he only had the future to worry about. The old Shane lived in a world where he didn't need to worry about anything.

Old me can't exist at TU. Not even in the name of not-so-wholesome fun.

The Shane that once existed is gone now. The Shane that needs to exist will be the kind of person who stays home on a Friday night and only goes on dates with guys he likes. The new Shane will not get wrapped up in drama and allow anyone to ruin his chance at a wonderful future.

New Shane and Old Shane are not the same.

For my entire life, I had planned on going to Yale, like my mom. Dartmouth was supposed to be my safe school. The one I fell back on if Yale fell through — and I didn't think it would back then — but it turns out that even Dartmouth doesn't want me.

Other schools didn't want me either. After Dartmouth rejected me, I focused on applying to as many schools as possible, but none of them would accept me. One after another, the rejections had poured in until I wasn't sure there was anywhere else for me to go.

This entire mess is all based on allegedly fake test scores. I didn't fake anything, but the powers that be still say I'm a cheater. So, here I am at TU because my uncle pulled more strings than I will ever be willing to admit.

He had swooped in when I needed him the most. High school graduation was only weeks away when he told me I would be able to attend TU.

This is one giant mess.

Fuck it. I take the path on the left, stuffing my hands in the pockets of my jeans.

What I have to do now is keep my head down and focus on getting good grades. Maybe if I change the school board's opinion of me, I might have another shot at Yale.

I can only hope.

I don't know what I'm going to do with my life if I can't get into Yale. Everything I had worked for through my last year of high school had been for nothing.

I sigh as I pass by a guy with a guitar sitting in a little courtyard. His shaggy hair falls into his eyes as he strums and hums to himself. He glances up for a moment, offering me a small smile. I think we share a class, but he looks like half of the other guys there. I nod in his direction before turning down another path.

Music rises up above the silence of the night. The stadium lights of the football field drown out the light from the stars. I pause on the hill that leads down to the open field, considering what a bad idea this is. If I'm caught anywhere near a party in the next few months, it will count as my one and only strike. Uncle James has made it perfectly clear I only get one chance.

"What do you think of that new band?" one girl asks her friend as they rush by me, teetering on too-tall heels. Her short skirt rises up, her heel catching in the path. Her friend reaches out to catch her before she can fall over.

I roll my eyes, watching as they descend into the party raging below. I want to go down and dance away my thoughts and fears, but the knowledge that my entire university life rides on the next few months keeps me glued in place. I can't do anything to ruin my chances.

I've already disappointed my mom enough.

Disappointing a dead woman is hard to do, but according to my uncle, I excel at it. Sometimes I consider what it would be like if I had just joined the army instead of coming to TU. I wouldn't need to do as my uncle said and I would be free to do as I choose.

As tempting as it is, I still want a college education. I don't want to keep letting my mom down. During high school, I took all the college-level classes I could, completing my first year of university credits before I had even graduated.

I worked hard over the summer, completing another year's worth of courses while I sat beside my dying mother in the hospital. I worked my ass off to get where I am and I'm not going to do anything to ruin my chance.

Mom thought it was crazy to try to complete two years' worth of courses before I even set foot in the university, but I saw it as a competition. The regular courses at high school hadn't challenged me enough. When I started acting out in classes, my guidance counselor pushed me to take advanced courses, thinking it would keep me busy.

It did, and between my junior year of high school and the summer before college, I didn't stop working. It challenged me and kept my mind off of my mom dying.

In the end, I at least had some college completed before she died. If she wasn't going to be around to see me graduate, I thought that having some advanced courses completed would be good enough.

Looking back on it now, I'm still happy I took all those courses, but it doesn't fix the pit I get in the bottom of my stomach when I think about my mom missing my graduation.

"I thought you weren't coming tonight," my roommate, Ethan, says as he appears beside me, a red plastic cup in his hand.

"Wasn't planning on it. Thought the party was at one of the fraternities?"

Ethan shrugs. "Campus security busted that. Instead of packing up, one of the guys from the football team decided the night was still young enough to keep partying."

I swing my gaze to where the party is taking place, half of me wishing I could join and the other half wanting to get as far away as possible. I shouldn't be here, and I know it.

"You going to come down and listen to some music?"

"It doesn't sound like a bad idea," I say, not wanting to turn Ethan down. The first month of getting to know each other has been rough. Ethan is quiet and keeps to himself, for the most part, his nose buried in a book. It makes getting to know a person difficult. To be honest, I'm surprised he's here since he seems to be an introvert.

"Cool," he says.

I can hear the music pounding through the speakers. It's some alternative rock with a good beat, but I don't think it's any band I've heard of before. I wouldn't mind staying longer and listening to the music. There's no harm in that, right?

If I'm smart, I'll turn around and head back to my dorm. I'll stay out of trouble, and I'll keep my head down. If I can make it through the next few months, I can make it through anything.

"Actually, I should be heading back to the dorm. I have a lot of reading I need to do for my economics class on Monday."

Ethan bobs his head to the beat of the music. "Alright."

As I turn to head back to my dorm, I catch sight of a lump beneath the bleachers to the right of the field. It's too dark to see much more than the lump, but the lights cast enough light beneath the bleachers to see a flash of blackberry-colored hair. It's not the greatest hiding place, especially if campus security or the cops show up, but it's better than nothing.

Go home. Go back to your dorm and go back to bed. A possibly drunk guy beneath the bleachers is not your problem.

While the guy isn't my problem, my mom raised me better than that. She would be disappointed in me if I left him alone. Yes, they are likely just drunk but there is something off about the entire scenario.

With a sigh, I head toward the still form and round the corner. The guy is attractive, there's no doubt about that. He looks like he belongs on a professional sports team rather than at a university, but who am I to judge?

I scan the area for any signs he was drinking alcohol or indulging in some kind of drug. No bottles litter the ground around him, and the breeze isn't wafting the stench of stale alcohol breath toward me. His breathing is shallow but steady. Clearly, he isn't like the other students celebrating the end of the first month of college.

"Hey, man." I crouch down beside him. "Are you alright?"

The guy groans and shifts his body slightly, his eyelids fluttering but never opening. I press my fingers against his neck, feeling a pulse and breathing a sigh of relief. Whatever is wrong with him isn't alcohol and he doesn't seem like he's about to die in front of me.

Somehow, I don't think the way the disciplinary committee sees me would ever be fixed if a student died while in my company.

"Hey, you good?" I shake his arm gently. "Sleeping here is a shitty idea."

The man rolls over, giving me a view of his full face, and the breath whooshes out of my lungs. For a minute, I consider leaving him here to sleep it off. Weston Perkins the Third. Perk the Jerk as he's known around campus. While he hasn't been rude to me personally, I hear rumors about him and the way he treats people.

From what I hear, he's the kind of person you leave to sleep alone under the bleachers. He's the kind of person you wouldn't think twice about if you were to walk away from him when he needed someone.

I know what it's like to be the guy everyone thinks horribly about. I suddenly feel bad for him. How many others have seen him like this and just left him because of who he is?

As much as I want to walk away, I'm better than that. With a sigh, I loop my arm behind his back and shove him upright. He groans again and mumbles something as I get him to his feet.

"Football players are heavy," I mutter, supporting most of his weight as I help him out from beneath the bleachers.

Perkins mumbles again, his head lolling to one side as I head in the direction of the dorms. Over the last month, I have really only seen him when he stumbles into the common area before heading to class in the mornings. Other than that, I might see him in our economics class occasionally, but the rest of the time, he's a ghost. I hear stories about him, though. They all say he's an arrogant ass who won't give anyone the time of day. He still manages to be popular though. I guess that's what being a star football player will get you. Must be nice.

As I drag Perkins toward the edge of the field, campus security descends on the party. Flashing lights surround the field and security officers race out of their cars toward the gathering. The music cuts off with a loud screech. People are shouting and running away, throwing their joints to the ground and stomping them out. Others seem completely unbothered by the risk of getting into trouble on school grounds.

"Shit." I look around. It's only a matter of time before security catches up to us. I spot a clump of bushes to the side. Whatever is wrong with Perkins doesn't seem to be life-threatening.

He groans as I lower him to the ground, trying to hide him in the shrubs. Once the branches are arranged to cover him, I turn and start walking away from the party. I'll come back for him once campus security has disappeared, but right now, the best thing I can do is to not be here.

"You there! Freeze!"

Cussing out Perkins in my head, I turn and look at the officer standing behind me. I offer the man a smile, but his eyes narrow.

"You're that problem kid they warned us about," he says slowly, looking me over. "I saw your picture in the office. It will thrill the dean to see you're in trouble already."

Goodbye Yale.

The security officer gestures to a car idling a few feet away. People are running around us, trying to escape the officers. Some of the party-goers scurrying across the field are clearly intoxicated, but the officer in front of me doesn't care. He's got his eyes set on a bigger prize.

The problem kid.

I sigh and follow him to the car, knowing there is no point in trying to run. No matter what happens next, my uncle will know I was at the party. I'll be lucky if he doesn't kick me out of school.

My heart pounds as I slide into the backseat of the campus security car. The officer says something into the radio before we begin the short drive to the dean's office.

Uncle James is going to kill me.

CHAPTER 2

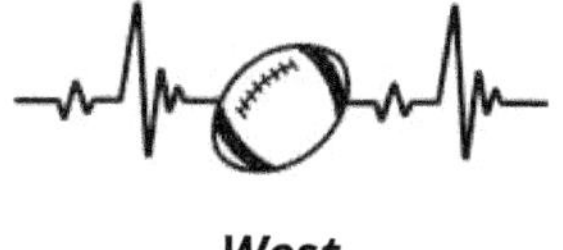

West

Sharp thorns are jabbing into my sides. With a groan, I roll over and open my eyes, hating how dry they feel. The beams of sunlight are so bright, I wince as they skim the parts of my skin that are exposed. A pounding headache overtakes my mind. It's not the kind of headache that comes from a night of drinking, though I wish it was. Overindulging in alcohol would have been a better explanation for why I'm in this position.

Where am I?

Leaves and branches surround me. I can hear people talking nearby. With my aching head, thinking about what happened the night before is nearly impossible. I remember taking a walk down to the party to listen to some music, but I don't remember much after that. Memories of people dancing and laughing flash through my head, but they are blurry at best.

Was I with anybody? Are they looking for me? Did they put me here?

I run a hand through my hair. A new band had been playing at the party when I got there. *Liquid Flames*. Word about them has been spreading throughout campus. Some of the guys on my team had been talking about them last week.

Liquid Flames drew me to the party, but why am I here?

I can't remember anyone leaving me in here. Hell, I don't remember talking to anybody at all. I could remember pulling up my hoodie and trying to blend into the crowd while listening to some good music. I tried avoiding the rest of the football team as much as possible. They were only interested in drinking. I only wanted to lose myself in the music, the good vibes.

With another groan, I crawl out of the bush only to see a campus security officer crouching down, looking for people? Probably. I watch as they drag a naked couple out of the bushes, tossing blankets over them before walking the pair to one of the security cars.

"Classy," I mutter as I stand up and brush the dirt from my jeans.

Though my mind is a little hazy, I stuff my hands in my pockets, knowing better than to appear as if I was one of the partiers. I walk away casually, keeping my head high and hopefully looking as if I had nothing to hide. None of the officers stop me.

When I get back to my dorm, there are people gathered in the common area. A table is littered with cups of black coffee and another person stumbles in and takes one.

I keep my head down as I head through the halls and up to my room. I have a private dorm on the top floor overlooking the courtyard. It's a nice enough place, though it's isolated from the others. Most days, I prefer it that way.

After entering my dorm, I strip down and head straight for the shower — another bonus of a private dorm. I don't have to share the bathroom with anyone else. My privacy is something that I keep hard boundaries on. I don't want to have anyone invading my space, or my life, no matter who they are.

My privacy is mine and mine alone.

***

The professor still isn't there when I walk into class an hour later. Thankfully, I'm able to slide into one of the seats in the back of the lecture hall. I stretch my legs out in front of me, dropping my backpack to the ground. As the last few people stagger into class, I open my backpack and pull out my laptop.

"Perkins," a guy says as he slides into the seat beside me.

I glance at him as he slouches in his seat a bit, shoving his hands in the pockets of his hoodie. His wavy light-brown hair falls into his eyes and they remind me of the Pacific Ocean, blue-green and stormy. There's a small dimple on his left cheek that I'm sure is more visible when he smiles. I find myself wanting to see that smile.

I'm trying to not be bothered by his scrutiny as he eyeballs me, but in the dark, dark recesses of my mind, I'm also trying not to admit that he's undeniably attractive.

Oh, fuck.

It's his penetrating stare that makes me uncomfortable. It's like he's trying to pull back the layers I've built around myself. When he looks at me like that, I might as well be naked.

"What?" I snap, wanting to slide down into my seat and become invisible. Instead, I sit taller and roll my shoulders back.

"So, the Jerk part is fitting," the guy says, the corner of his mouth twitching upward. "One would think that you would try to change that reputation."

I hate my nickname around campus, though I know it's well-deserved. Somehow, the name seems worse coming from him than it does from anyone else. I don't know why I care about his opinion, especially so soon after meeting him, but I don't want him to hate me.

I can't let him know that, though. I have a horrible reputation to uphold, and what he's looking for likely isn't going to happen.

I sigh. "What do you want?"

"Well, a thank you for starters. If I hadn't stuffed your ass in the bushes, campus security would have busted us both. Instead, my ass is the one on the line with the dean."

"How is that my problem?" I ask before looking away from him and opening up a new document on my laptop. "You're the reason I woke up getting stabbed by thorns. That thank you isn't going to happen."

"Wow. You really are a piece of work, aren't you?"

The guy shakes his head as the professor walks into the room. I breathe a sigh of relief, grateful he has no choice but to stop talking to me about whatever happened last night. The last thing I want is to talk about why I passed out on a football field.

With any other person, I would have been able to claim I was drunk. They would believe it too. The star tight end of TU's football team drinking himself into a stupor after a game wouldn't have surprised anyone. This guy had been closer to me, though. He would have been able to smell the alcohol on me if I'd been drinking, and I hadn't had a drop.

I try to find an excuse that might be believable, but none come to mind. Drinking is already ruled out and if I told him I was using drugs — which I'm not — it would get back to Coach and he would kick me off the team. Everything I've worked so hard for would be ripped away from me in the blink of an eye.

Instead of giving him an explanation, I ignore him.

"So, why were you passed out under the bleachers?" His voice is low as I peek over at him. He's staring at the slides being projected onto the screen, not bothering to look at me as he speaks.

I want to disappear. I want a large hole to rip open beneath my desk and pull me down into the depths of hell just so I can avoid this conversation.

"I don't know what you're talking about." I stare at the notes being displayed. "Now, get lost. I'm trying to pay attention to the lecture and you're making it difficult."

"Interesting." I can hear the amusement in his voice. "You would think that knowing I got in trouble after saving your ass would make you feel indebted to me."

"You're the idiot that chose to drag me around instead of running like the rest of the intelligent people. Who sees campus security and thinks they should help someone else, a stranger no less, instead of avoiding getting caught?"

The guy chuckles. "Good to know this is all a joke to you. Next time, I won't go checking on you to see if you need an ambulance or anything."

"Nobody asked you to check on me in the first place. I'm a grown man and can take care of myself."

"Says the guy who was passed out under the bleachers."

We fall silent as the professor finishes writing notes on the slides and starts his lecture. He walks back and forth in front of the room, talking about measuring macroeconomic data, and all I can think about is the guy sitting beside me.

I should thank him, but I can't bring myself to do it. If I acknowledge I needed his help last night, he might start asking more questions about what happened.

Even if I wanted to tell him, I couldn't. I don't know what happened either. One moment I felt fine. The music was good, and I was successfully avoiding the rest of the football team. When Liquid Flames stepped back for a break, I had gone for a walk to clear my head of everything that was starting to pile up in it. The next thing I know, I'm waking up covered in dirt and grass with no memory of how I got there.

"My name's Shane, just in case you ever decide you want to thank me," the guy says quietly, keeping his voice low as the professor continues to drone on. "Personally, I would think thanking someone, maybe even going with them to talk to the dean about what happened last night, would be a pretty good idea."

"I don't even know who you are. I don't remember seeing you last night at all. Why would I claim to know what you were doing there and why if it's not true?"

From the corner of my eye, I see Shane nod. That easy-going smile is still spread across his face, even if there is a glimmer of irritation starting to appear. He clenches his pen, his knuckles turning white as he takes down notes.

"I don't think I'm asking for much," Shane says when the professor pauses to drink some water. "I saved your ass; I think you can save mine. After that, we can go our separate ways and never have to talk to each other ever again."

"I'd rather not get involved."

Shane sighs. "Whatever."

Silence falls over him again as the professor resumes his lecture. I type quickly, keeping detailed notes. The football coach requires a good GPA from all his players, with no exceptions. He's the kind of coach who accepts nothing less than excellence in all areas of education. His team is not there just to play football — he won't allow that to be our mentality.

School has never come as easily to me as it did with my siblings, and I knew it bothered my parents. I work twice as hard as my brother and sister to maintain the same sort of grades they had. Still, I hold my own at school and I was able to leave high school with high honors.

It's just maintaining those honors that exhausts me.

"Twenty minutes. That's all I need from you and then you can go on with your life."

"Man, just piss off and leave me alone, alright?" I say as the bell rings, signaling the end of the class. "I already told you that I'm not doing shit."

Shane flips me his middle finger before gathering his things and leaving. I sit for a few moments longer, skimming through my notes. There are a few seconds right after he leaves when I consider chasing after him and telling him that I'll help.

Instead, I gather my own belongings and head to my next class.

Chapter 3

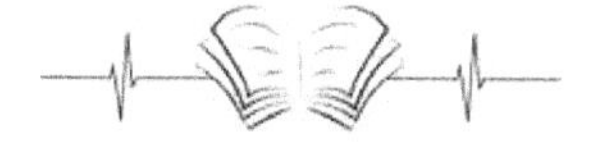

Shane

I can only think of one, possibly two things, I hate more than talking to Uncle James. One of those things is talking to Uncle James when he's acting as Dean James, the tight ass at TU — and I don't mean that in a complimentary way.

Uncle James is the kind of man that most of the family forgets to invite to the annual Christmas party. At least, they all claim that they forgot, even though everybody knows they didn't. Each year, without fail, Uncle James will still show up just to tell everyone else that he is better than them using subtle jabs.

But I have to admit, when I needed him most, he stepped in. I still don't think that had anything to do with helping me, but more to do with his rubbing it in Mom's face that he could help me while she couldn't. That he could step in and fix my future with the snap of his fingers while her Yale education did nothing for her. She was dying in a hospital bed and he was fixing my life with nothing more than a couple of words to the people he works with.

I want to hate him for it, but without him, I wouldn't have a chance to do right by my mom. I wouldn't have the chance to honor her memory and get the education she always dreamed of for me.

Even though Uncle James stepped in to help, saving my education is about him more than it is about me.

I look around his office as I sit in one of the chairs, waiting to hear what he has to say. When campus security dragged me here last night, Uncle James was nowhere to be found. Instead, his secretary scheduled a meeting and told me to show up on time, as if I was ever late.

The doors bang open as Uncle James walks in, his signature frown set deep on his forehead. I'm already preparing myself for the lecture of a lifetime when he sits down across from me and crosses one leg over the other.

Talking to Perkins earlier had gotten me nowhere. There had been nothing but a void expression in those honey-gold eyes of his. If he wasn't such a jerk, I might have considered asking him out for a drink, but the moment he opened his mouth, the attraction I felt for him diminished. There is still a lingering curiosity, but I'm not going there. Not if he can't even be bothered to have a short conversation with my uncle to explain what happened.

Any kind of decent person would have come with me, or at the very least written some kind of note or made a call to explain that I had saved their ass. Not Perk the Jerk though.

Self-absorbed prick. Attractive but a self-absorbed prick.

He's beautiful to look at. Tall, perhaps half a foot taller than my six-foot frame. Broad shoulders, powerful thighs, warm brown eyes framed by ridiculously long, beautiful eyelashes. A perennial three-day stubble. Perkins is just too handsome for his own good.

But I'll be damned if I get caught up in the way he looks on the outside and forget he isn't called The Jerk for no reason. He is literally a jerk on the inside.

"I have to say," Uncle James says slowly, jolting me from my thoughts, and clearly working up to whatever brilliant speech he has masterminded this time. "I thought better of you, Shane. I thought by putting my own name on the line, you would get your act together here and work on turning your life around. I was certain that improving yourself was the point of your probationary period."

"I thought that it was because the school board believed I faked my test scores."

Uncle James sighs. "Shane, let's not get into this argument again. I'm not interested in whether or not you did the unthinkable. Even though we both know you probably did. What matters is that you start figuring out what you want out of life instead of slumming around at parties and looking to get into more trouble."

"Uncle, I wasn't drinking at that party. I was out for a walk after the meeting with the disciplinary committee. I heard some music and went to listen to it for a few minutes. I didn't drink. I didn't do anything wrong."

I'm not sure why I don't tell him about dragging Perkins from beneath the bleachers. Something about it just doesn't feel like it's my story to tell, so I leave it out.

Besides, my uncle would only hear the part about me being under the bleachers with Perkins. He'll then assume Perkins is on drugs, and if I'm under the bleachers with him, I must be, too.

It seems extreme, even when I play it out in my mind. However, after years of dealing with my uncle's bullshit, even the extreme is likely.

"They placed you on probation hours before being caught at the party, Shane. You don't think that I am just going to overlook this, do you? Because I can't. You are already being watched by the members of the committee, which means I'm being watched as well. They know you're my nephew. If it seems like I'm going too easy on you, we'll both be in more trouble."

"I know."

Uncle James uncrosses his legs so he can cross them the other way. "We have to do something. You were not caught drinking and the officer said you didn't smell like you had been. My secretary confirmed that you were alert when you were brought in last night. That leads me to believe at least part of your story is true."

I resist the urge to roll my eyes and instead lean further back in my seat. Trying to argue with him when he's already decided on a narrative won't fix anything. My uncle is nothing if not a stubborn man. Once he has his mind made up about something, he isn't likely to change it.

"It's only the first month of school and I know that with all the activities that are coming up, students are excited. Plus, our football team is looking better than ever. You weren't drinking. Instead of recommending disciplinary action from the committee, I'm going to put a curfew in place. Midnight on the weekends. Eleven through the week. I'll be instructing your RA to check in on you at curfew."

My hands tighten around the arms of the chair. I want to start arguing with him, but it won't do me any good. He has made up his mind about what kind of person I am. I can already tell that isn't going to change.

"Thank you," I say, knowing that it's the only response he will expect and accept.

"Don't make any more mistakes, Shane. There's only so much I can do to protect you." My uncle stands and walks me to the door. "I don't want to send you back home, so keep in line from now on."

"I understand. Thank you," I say again, walking out of his office.

As soon as his door slams shut behind me, I unclench my fists and roll my shoulders. That could have gone a hell of a lot worse than it did. I could have been looking at an immediate end to my time at TU.

Allegedly faked test scores and an expulsion would keep me from getting into another school. To be frank,

I need to get into another school. TU isn't as impressive on a resume as Yale.

I keep my head down as I leave the administration building and make my way toward the dorms. I've got to go over my economics notes and try to study for a test in one of my other classes that's coming up.

The sun is starting to dip below the horizon as I approach my building, the wind rustling the leaves in the trees. I sit down on the front steps, watching as people rush to and from their last classes of the day. Running my hands through my hair, I try to figure out how I am going to handle the rest of the semester. While Uncle James got me into the school, I have a feeling he's also looking to kick me out. Another step in proving to my mom he's better than she is. It doesn't matter to him that she's dead and gone. He still acts like he has something to prove.

I've been a pawn in his game of one-upmanship for far too long and it tears me in half that it continues even after her death.

Feeling tired from people watching, I rise from the steps and stretch my stiff limbs. After slipping on my hoodie, joggers, and a pair of lightweight trainers, I hit the tracks. Today is all about speed. Maybe I'll be able to outrun the mess that is my life.

Running has always been a means to clear my head and with the shit that has been piling on me lately, I definitely need to run, right the fuck now. About an hour later, feeling more invigorated than when I started, I slow down to a walk and check my watch.

Good. I've shaved off a couple of seconds from my time during that last sprint. And I feel like I have restored my equilibrium...but my breathing is still somewhat accelerated.

I walk around to the back of the dorm where the staircase leads up to the top floor, across the hall from my room. Fewer people take this route, meaning more time without having to plaster on a fake smile and pretend like my life isn't a complete shit show.

As I turn the corner of the building, I see a mop of hair, the color of ripe blackberries, attached to an annoying football player laying at the bottom of the stairs.

"Perfect," I mutter under my breath as I walk over to him. Just what I need to be dealing with right now. I should just leave him here to figure things out on his own.

A brief stab of curiosity flows through me as I look down at him. There's got to be something wrong with me. How can I justify wanting to care for this man, putting his needs before my own, and he doesn't give two shits about me?

Instead of thinking about whatever strange feelings are rising, I stuff them back down and crouch beside Perkins. I see the rise and fall of his chest, but still press my fingers against his neck, looking for a steady pulse. When I find one, I pull back and stare at him.

Drool leaves a trail from the corner of his lips down his cheek, and his eyes have rolled back in his head. There's a cut on his forehead, which doesn't look deep, possibly from hitting his head on the way down. I sigh and gently maneuver him into a sitting position.

"Perkins, we can't keep meeting like this." My voice is light as I lightly tap my fingers on his cheek. I'm relieved to see that he's more alert than he was just a few minutes ago. "You have to stop throwing yourself to the ground every time I come around. It's starting to look desperate, man. How would the rest of your teammates feel if they knew you were literally falling head over heels for me?"

"Not funny," Perkins mutters, his words slurring together as his eyelids flutter. "Go away."

"Nice way to talk to the guy who keeps rescuing you." I wave my hand in front of his face. Though his eyes are heavy-lidded, he does follow my movements. "I'm going to call an ambulance."

"No!" Perkins shouts, his voice stronger than it was before. "No ambulance. Leave me here. I'll be fine in a few minutes."

"Brilliant idea. Smash your head on the way down the stairs and then ask to be left here to deal with a head injury on your own. That's smart."

Before he can say anything else, his eyes are rolling back in his head again and his body lurches. I lunge forward and catch him before he hits the ground. Perkins is heavy and being unconscious and limp only makes it worse. After taking a deep breath, I adjust my hold on him and haul him up.

He groans, his head slumping onto my shoulder. I look around, but nobody is around to help. Even though I run and work out at the gym on occasion, it still doesn't mean I can easily lift him, since he's packed with muscle.

"Guess I'll have to carry you," I say, tightening my grip around his waist.

Perkins moves slightly, shuffling his feet on the ground. "Help."

"Nearly polite," I say as I help him step up, supporting most of his weight.

"Shush."

"So polite."

It takes a long time to get up the stairs. For each step I take, it seems as if it takes a thousand more for Perkins. He slips in and out of consciousness, his words slurring together when he's alert. As I help him up the stairs, I study him for signs of drugs or alcohol. Other than passing out, he doesn't seem to be under the influence.

My stomach twists and everything in me says I should call the ambulance, but when I remember his panic at mentioning one, I still don't call. I have no idea what the plan is beyond just getting to his dorm room and not letting him die.

We get to the top floor, and I head just past my room to his. He lives at the end of the hallway, one of the few private dorms in the building. Ethan had pointed it out a few days ago in an offhand comment that he wished he were lucky enough to have one of those.

I lean Perkins against the wall, searching through his pockets for his keys. When I find them, I unlock the door and push it open before helping him inside. He groans as we stumble to his bed. I help him sit down on the edge before taking a step back.

"Are you going to be alright?" I tuck my hands into my pockets as Perkins rolls further onto his bed and buries his face in his pillow. "Are you sure you don't want me to call an ambulance? You don't look so good."

"Mind your business," he mumbles, reaching for his blanket and pulling it up around him.

For a moment, I consider leaving him to fend for himself, but I'm still on the fence about leaving him. He doesn't look like he's going to get better any time soon, but I'm not sure what else I can do.

I glance around the room, seeing a couple of pill bottles on his desk and a doctor's note taped to the mini-fridge. Instead of snooping through his things like I want to do, I shake my head and look at him.

There's nothing else I can do to help him and even if I could, I'm not sure I would. He hasn't done anything to deserve it. Normally I wouldn't expect a thank you after helping someone, but with how he's treating me, as if I'm the piece of shit he stepped on while wearing his five-hundred-dollar Golden Goose sneakers, I feel like I should get out of his room and mind my business, stat.

"This is pathetic. Get yourself together and stop being an ass to the people that are helping you," I say before walking out of his room and slamming the door behind me.

Next time, I'll call an ambulance and leave him to deal with his own mess, since he clearly doesn't want my help.

Chapter 4

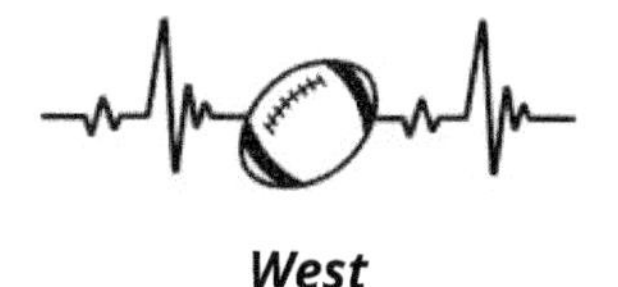

West

I stand at the front of the lecture hall, my backpack slung over my shoulder. I can see Shane sitting in the far corner, his head bent over his desk as he reads from his tablet. His champagne-blond hair is hanging over his face and for a moment, I consider walking over to him and brushing the hair from his face.

What the fuck?

I would brush a girlfriend's hair out of her face, not some random guy I barely knew and had been unbelievably rude to.

Thoughts continue to swirl around in my head. The worry etched on Shane's face as he put me into bed last night, followed closely by disgust is burned into my mind. I don't want him to be disgusted by me, but I don't know what else to do. If it were up to me, I would have woken up exactly where I passed out. Then I wouldn't feel like I owed anybody anything.

Shaking the thought from my head, I walk across the room to him. There's something I need to do, whether or not I feel comfortable doing it. And besides, my mother would be upset if she knew how I've treated Shane, especially after he's done nothing but help me.

Although, I think she would be more upset if she knew that I was passing out randomly amidst strangers. She would be worried about all the things that could happen to me.

"Hey," I say, sitting down in the seat beside Shane and dropping my bag to the floor. "Can we talk?"

"Sure," Shane says, his tone clipped. He doesn't look up at me and for some reason, that bothers me even more than his tone.

I thought he would be interested in talking to me. Clearly, he isn't. In fact, if the tense set of his shoulders is anything to go by, he wants me to go away. But I can't do that until I apologize for my behavior.

Get yourself together. You're tired and not thinking straight. Say what you need to say and then stay away from Shane.

"Great," I say, shifting in my seat. "Thank you for having my back. I don't know what would have happened if you weren't there to save my ass."

"Yeah, whatever." He continues reading from his tablet.

"That's it? After going off on me about how you got in trouble, *yeah whatever* is all you have to say?" I scoff and roll my eyes. "I expected more."

"Yeah, whatever," he says in the same monotone voice.

Shane still doesn't look up. I frown at him, wondering what crawled up his ass, before grabbing my backpack off the floor and moving to the other side of the room. Anderson looks up from his phone, a frown on his face.

"What's happening?" I ask as I sit down beside him and pull out my laptop.

"Nothing. Some girl I was with the other weekend is being clingy and I can't seem to shake her. She showed up at my dorm the other night and Liam nearly threw a fit."

I laugh and shake my head. "When doesn't Liam throw a fit? Why don't you just ask for another room assignment?"

"And end up with somebody worse?" Anderson asks, his fingers flying across the screen. "No thanks. At least with Liam, I know what to expect."

The professor enters the room and drops a stack of files on his desk. He sips the coffee in his hand slowly as he starts the projector and sorts through his notes. As he prepares for the lecture, I glance over at Shane again. He keeps his head bent over some papers this time, a hard set to his jaw. There's another twist of guilt in my stomach as I wonder how I can fix what I broke.

He doesn't give off the vibe that he's a jerk or anything like that. I hate to admit it, but I've been an asshole to him. Obviously, he's nice enough, as evidenced by the fact that he's helped me on a number of occasions in spite of how stupidly I've reacted. I just don't have time to deal with anything else in my life. I barely have time for all the people, classes, and football as it is.

Then there are the weekly breakfasts with my mother and calling my siblings a couple of times a week. We all try to stay in contact with each other, even when life gets busy. With everything that I have piled on my plate, I don't have time for another complication like Shane.

When the professor starts his lecture, I follow along. Every now and then, I can feel eyes on me, but when I glance over, Shane has already looked away — if he was even looking at me in the first place.

I just want to go play football and have a nap.

***

Coach Veer blows his whistle, calling the team to a stop. Sweat is dripping down my face as I run from the end zone to centerfield. The team gathers in a circle around Coach, our chests heaving as we wait for him to start speaking.

He's a good man, dedicated to the game and his team. One of the reasons I wanted to come to TU was because of him. He's one of the university coaches that high schools talk about, and he's revered. He's the kind of coach that takes players to the NFL. He creates success stories.

The sun is shining high overhead, the day unusually warm for October. I'm sweating more than usual in my uniform, as are most of the other guys. One of the team assistants passes around bottles of water.

Coach looks at all of us, his playbook clutched against his side. He presses his mouth into a thin line, a sign of his disappointment. The guys around me shift their weight from one foot to another as they drink their water, their eyes never leaving our coach.

"We're going to scrimmage today. Divide yourselves into two teams and start running the modified plays from the last game. I don't want to keep seeing losses like the one we had against the Bulldogs." Coach fixes his eyes on each member of the team, one player at a time.

I resist the urge to squirm. Coach can be quite intimidating.

"Are you ready?" his voice booms.

"Yes, Coach!" we yell in unison before splitting apart.

In a well-practiced routine, we separate ourselves into two teams and the team captain calls the plays as we get into position. I tilt my head from side to side, stretching out the muscles. I'm more tired today than I usually am, even though all we've done is warmups.

We break and I take off ahead of the quarterback, watching for the players who come racing our way. I tackle one, groaning as our bodies slam against the ground. Coach blows his whistle and the play comes to an end as he marches onto the field.

I stand up and roll my shoulders, trying to loosen up as I take off my helmet. Coach stops in front of me, his arms crossed and his eyebrows furrowing. I can tell what's coming before he even starts to speak. I'm not playing as well as I usually do and it's showing.

"What was that, Perkins?" His tone is sharp. "Where is your head at? It sure as hell doesn't look like it's out on the field with the rest of your team."

"Sorry, Coach," I try to ignore the sympathetic looks I know I'm getting from my teammates.

"I don't want to hear you're sorry, Perkins. Get your head in the game. If this were an actual game, your team would be falling behind. Your tackle was weak and your opponent was back up in seconds and running after your quarterback. It's your job to protect him."

"Yes, Coach."

He nods and looks around at the rest of the team. "Back to the scrimmage," he tells the guys, and then he pins his eyes on me. "Perkins, a moment."

I wait as the rest of the team clears out and heads back onto the field. Coach turns to me, his expression still hard. My stomach twists in knots. I like disappointing Coach as much as I like poking an angry bear right after hibernation.

"My office after practice."

"Yes, Coach."

Second to actual games, there's nothing I like more than football practice and the pain that comes along with it. Football is easy. All I have to do is keep fit and focused, and run the plays. There's nothing else that matters when I'm on the field. It's just me and my team. None of the other shit going on in my life matters at that moment.

Football is the only thing in my life that makes sense. It makes me feel like I know who I am.

I head back to the field when Coach nods and walks away. For the rest of our practice, all I feel is exhaustion. My muscles ache and my joints are sore. Every time I move, I can hear another joint crack.

Jogging off the field, my teammates turn right to head to their lockers, while I take the left down another hall to the coach's office. The door is open, and Coach is sitting behind his desk. I keep my helmet clutched in my hand, the mouth guard hanging from it.

"Perkins, come in and take a seat," Coach says, looking up from whatever note he was writing in the playbook. I'm sure that note will make an appearance at our next practice in the form of a shouted criticism.

I nod, my heart racing in my chest. Everything about this feels wrong, like somehow he knows something that he shouldn't. Thoughts of being kicked off the team flood my mind. The room seems as if it's getting smaller, the walls of Coach's office starting to close in around me.

Drawing his eyebrows together, he asks, "Perkins, son, are you alright? You're pale."

His concern for me is obviously genuine.

"Fine." My voice is barely more than a squeak. "I'm fine."

"What happened out there today?" Leaning in toward his desk and making a steeple with his fingers, Coach continues, "You weren't playing like you usually do. You're one of the players I can count on to always have your head in the game. You're going to be scouted at the next game and likely followed throughout the season after that."

"I am?" Hope soars in my chest. Being scouted by the NFL was everything I had ever hoped for. It's the reason why I worked so hard at being good at football.

Nodding his head, Coach confirms, "You are. I've heard from several teams that they have people coming to our games to see you and a couple of the other players. You've got this, Perkins. This opportunity is yours to lose. Your future in the sport depends on you."

Everything I've ever wanted is starting to line up in front of me. I can't do anything to risk my success with the team. If I want to make it to the NFL — and I really fucking do — I need to focus on my goal and avoid distractions. I can't let anything else matter to me when I'm out on that field.

I swallow hard and nod. "I understand, Coach. It won't happen again. I'm fine."

"Are you sure? We can have one of the campus doctors over here in a few minutes to check you out."

The world around me freezes at the mention of the campus doctor. I plaster on a smile and shake my head, hoping I'm acting the way I normally do and not about to fall into a deep spiral of panic. Coach can't call the doctor.

There isn't anything wrong with me. I'm doing fine. I'm just tired and it was hot on the field.

"No need to call the doctor," I say, getting up and backing toward the door. "I'm fine, Coach. Just an off day. There was a lot of work in my economics class today and I'm still processing some of it."

Coach doesn't look as if he believes me, but he doesn't press the matter either. Instead, he nods and goes back to flipping through his playbook.

It's his standard dismissal and I'm not about to stick around any longer for him to change his mind.

I nearly run from his office to the lockers, my head spinning as I go. Everything feels as if it's in slow-motion. I peel off my uniform and stuff it into the laundry cart by the showers. Most of the other players have left, but Maddox and Anderson are still lingering by their lockers and talking about assignments in one of their classes.

"You alright, man?" Anderson asks, looking over at me as I stumble to the shower with a towel wrapped around my waist.

"Fine. Just tired. Long night last night. Long day."

Maddox raises an eyebrow and crosses his arms. "Are you sure?"

I wave them off and enter one of the shower stalls, cranking the water as hot as it will go. "Completely fine. I'll be in here for a while, so see you later?"

"Yeah," Anderson says, his voice hesitant. "See you later."

I wait until I hear the locker room doors slam shut before getting to work scrubbing the sweat from my body. My head is still spinning as I sway on my feet. After a few sways, I get out of the shower and sit down on one of the benches.

I'm not doing alright.

I reach into my locker across from the bench and pull out a change of clothes.

I can't let anybody know what's going on. Coach will bench me.

Chapter 5

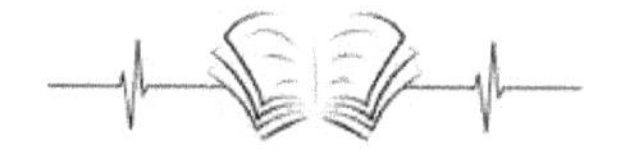

Shane

Ignoring Perkins for the last two weeks has been much harder than I thought it would be initially. For the first month of school, I didn't notice that he lingered in the back of most of my classes with his friends.

Now, it's the middle of October and I notice him every time we're in the same room together. It happens a lot. We share more classes than I thought we did, which is both good and bad.

I don't want to notice him, but he makes it impossible not to. There's something about the way his hair falls, a mess he clearly didn't intend, that has me wanting to run my fingers through it. Which will definitely never happen since, as far as I know, Perkins is not into men, let alone me. Still, it's hard for me not to like the intensity of his amber-brown eyes. And don't even get me started on the width of his shoulders and the confidence in his gait. They're hard to resist.

I'm still not sure how to feel about that. On one hand, there's a reason why he's known as Perk the Jerk around campus. Couple that with the fact that I'm supposed to be staying out of trouble, and there are a million reasons why I shouldn't be interested.

Other than his looks, there aren't many reasons why I should be interested. I'm not usually a fickle guy who's intensely attracted to someone's looks without getting to know them better. But there's something about Perkins that gets me going.

I don't know him and I'm not going to pretend that I do. From everything I've seen so far, he's the typical football player. He and his dumb friends sit around and act like arrogant assholes who think all those who aren't on the team are beneath them.

But then there's something in those fleeting glances where our eyes meet across the room. I can see the curiosity in his gaze before he looks away again. He seems to be teetering on the edge of something, and there's a dark part of me that hopes to see the moment when he falls off the edge.

As the door opens to the lecture hall again, I look up and see Perkins strolling in. He's laughing and bumping his shoulder into one of his friends. I glance away from them and stare down at the papers in front of me. Only half of my notes make sense. The rest look like they're written in a foreign language, even though I know I'm the one who wrote them.

"Hey." Ethan slides into the seat beside me. "Any big plans for Halloween yet?"

"Just keeping myself out of trouble," I say, flipping to a blank page and pulling a pen out of my backpack. "I don't really like parties and I have some assignments due in my other class."

"Well, if you change your mind, there's going to be a big party down Greek Row. The fraternities and sororities are throwing some sort of costume party. A few of my friends and I will be going, and you're welcome to join us."

"Thanks, man," I say with a grin. I appreciate the invitation, but I have no desire to go to a party. "I appreciate it, but I really do have a bunch of things I need to get done."

"No worries," Ethan says with an easy smile, getting up and going to join his friends on the other side of the room.

Even though Ethan and I share a dorm, I still wasn't telling him about the probation I was on with the disciplinary committee. The more people who knew, the better behavior I would have to be on. I just want to be with people who I can be myself around. People who won't think I did something wrong just because the school board insists that I did.

I watch Perkins throughout class. While he's kind to his friends, he glares at the people around him. There's something about the vacant look in his eyes when he glares that makes me wonder if he even knows he's doing it. Maybe all that medication I saw is turning him into someone he's not.

That thought leaves me as soon as a guy trips over Perkins's backpack and falls. Perkins shakes his head and lightly pushes his backpack out of the way as the guy sputters and gets to his feet, clearly embarrassed judging by the flush creeping across his cheeks. Perkins's friend says something too quiet for me to hear, but all I can feel is disgust.

What kind of person treats someone like that, with not even an apology, even if they are on medication?

I don't care what's wrong with him. There's no excuse to treat another person like they're less than you.

I shake my head and lean back in my seat, stretching my legs out in front of me and hoping the class ends soon.

***

My stomach is growling as I walk into the dining hall, the scent of tacos and burritos wafting through the air. I grin and make my way to the buffet, ready for something to eat. As I wait in line, I look around the room for an empty seat. There aren't many, but I'm not surprised. Taco day brings in most of the students for dinner.

Once my tacos are lined up neatly on my plate, I go to the exit that leads to the outdoor tables. It isn't a particularly nice day out, so I'm hoping there's an empty table where I can be alone to do some reading.

There's a table in a corner, nicely tucked away and secluded. I hurry to it, swinging my backpack off my shoulder onto the ground before sliding into a seat. I put my plate on the table and dig in. My first taco is halfway into my mouth when I hear someone coughing and choking.

As much as my stomach wants me to ignore it and continue eating, I can't. I grab my bag, get up, and hurry around the side of the building, in the direction of the coughing, and see Perkins doubled over.

Spatters of blood are on the ground in front of him and more is coming up as he coughs.

Dark crimson spots appear on the front of his shirt as he coughs again, more blood hitting the ground and his clothes. I watch for a moment as others pass by, none of them seem to notice what's happening. Maybe they do notice but maybe he has done something to wrong them in the past. Maybe they know there's something wrong with him, but they're ignoring it because of the way he treats people.

There is a brief moment where I consider walking away and leaving him to fend for himself. He has made it abundantly clear more than once that he doesn't want my help. Still, coughing up blood is never a good thing, and everything comes to a standstill when I see him in pain. Perkins coughs again, more blood spraying onto the ground.

"What's wrong with you, man?" I rest my hand on his shoulder against my better judgment. Tingles race through my body at the slight touch, but Perkins jerks away and glares at me.

Here we go again.

I shake my head. I'm tired of dealing with his attitude every time I find him looking like he's on the verge of death.

"Don't touch me."

"Fine, whatever," I say, stepping back from him and holding my hands up. "Help yourself then."

Perkins flips me off before his hands go to his knees and his body starts shaking when he coughs again. Blood trickles down the side of his mouth and his face turns a bright shade of red.

"Are you sure there's nothing I can do to help?"

Wiping away the blood from his mouth with the sleeve of his sweater, he says, "I don't need your help. Not even a little. Go away, Shane."

"Fine. Have a nice life, Perkins."

As I turn, I can hear him start coughing again. My steps are slow and measured as I walk away, waiting for what I know is coming. No matter how much he hates me, there's no denying he needs help.

"Wait," Perkins says finally, his voice raspy. "Wait."

I spin on my heel and walk back to him, crossing my arms over my chest. "What?"

"Don't go."

"What's wrong with you?" I ask as he begins coughing again. "Coughing up blood isn't normal. We need to take you to the campus doctor."

"No. Mind your own business," Perkins says, shaking his head with panic clear in his eyes. "I'm not going to a doctor."

"This is ridiculous. I've got other things I need to be doing."

Perkins coughs again, dropping to his knees as the energy seems to leave his body. I crouch down beside him, but he shakes his head and flips me off.

Typical.

"Nice. Real nice. I can see why they call you a jerk. It's really a shame. I was hoping everybody was wrong about you, but clearly, they're not. Have fun coughing up a lung. Who should I call about your apparent death wish?"

"I told you to mind your own business," he says between coughing fits.

"I will."

Perkins starts swaying, his head drooping lower and lower. As much as I want to walk away, I wrap my arm around his waist and drape his arm over my shoulders. Perkins is coughing too much to say anything as I lift him to his feet.

There's no way I can leave him here like this, as much as I might want to. If I were in the same position — even if I was acting like an ass — I would still want someone to stop and help me. I would be scared about what's happening and I would need someone to tell me that everything's going to be okay.

Maybe that's why I decide to help him again, even though he doesn't want me to. I don't want to leave him here to deal with this crisis on his own.

"Clinic. In. Town." He struggles to catch his breath, his words broken up by coughs. Perkins fumbles around in the pocket of his jeans before handing me a key fob. He barely has enough strength to tell me the color, model, and license plate number of his car.

"Student lot?" I ask, already walking us in that direction.

Perkins nods, holding his fist to his mouth as he coughs. I see blood spots appear on his hand, bright crimson against the pale skin.

As we walk, I try not to let the way he holds onto me affect me. My racing heart gives me away as I hobble down the path, carrying most of Perkins's weight. I curse the attraction I feel as if it's a living thing, a separate entity. In my mind, I'm shoving Perkins away from me, so I can go somewhere else to clear my head.

By the time we reach the parking lot, Perkins is barely conscious. His head hangs low, and his arm is limp against me. I struggle with his weight as I unlock his car before helping him inside. Once he's settled and his seat belt is on, I jog around to the other side of the car and get in. Perkins slumps against the door, his eyes half-closed as I peel out of the parking lot and head toward town.

***

Perkins is whisked away to one of the rooms as soon as I drag him inside the clinic. The nurses seem to recognize him, insisting on pulling his file and calling for a specific doctor. I watch from the waiting room as they work quickly and a doctor comes running down the hall, her white lab coat flying out behind her.

Taking a seat in one of the plush chairs near the window, I stretch my legs out in front of me. Perkins isn't the kind of man who'd want me to wait, but I don't want to leave either. I need to see that he's going to be okay and nothing is horribly wrong with him. As I wait, I take out my phone and google all the reasons a person would cough up blood. With each additional reason I read, my stomach sinks a little closer to my feet.

The clock on the wall ticks in a steady rhythm. Each time I look at it, I see another minute of a class I'm missing go by. One class begins and ends before the next starts and I'm still waiting. Uncle James isn't going to be happy when he hears I skipped two classes in one day.

Surely his little campus spies will tell him.

I don't like being watched. If I had my say in the matter, I would go to a school in the middle of nowhere where nobody had ever heard of my uncle.

Since the last meeting with Uncle James, I've been noticing more professors watching me. Their eyes follow me everywhere, as if waiting for me to make a mistake so they can run and report it to my uncle. With possibly an entire staff watching me, the slightest step out of line will be caught and reported to him.

Not much makes him happy though, so even though I'm annoyed he'll find out, I'm not too worried about it.

After another hour has gone by, I see the doctor leave the room Perkins was in. She has a stack of papers in her hands and several vials filled with blood. One of the nurses heads inside the room.

What I wouldn't give to be a fly on that wall. I know it's wrong to invade someone's privacy, but Perkins is hiding something, and I've always been a curious person. I want to know what I keep risking my future over.

Even if I ask him, I know he won't tell me. Maybe it's easier to keep my mouth shut and just watch him. If he thinks I'm not worrying about what's wrong with him, he might be more likely to slip up and make a mistake that gives me a hint as to what's going on.

A few more minutes pass before Perkins comes out of the room. The blood stains have now darkened on his shirt, and there are bags underneath his eyes. He glances around the waiting room, a look I can't quite comprehend passing over his face before he settles into a deep frown. He approaches me with his hands in his pockets, staring at the ground.

"Do you want to talk about it?" I ask as I stand up.

Perkins looks up at me and shakes his head. "Not even a little bit."

"Alright then, I just thought you might want to give some sort of explanation to the person that just missed two classes to haul you into town to see a doctor, but I guess I was wrong."

"Well shit," Perkins says slowly, a smirk on his face as he leads the way to the door. "It looks like you're finally learning."

"Listen here, asshole," I say the moment we're outside. Perkins turns to face me, that smirk still on his face. "This is twice I've risked my chance at a fucking future. The least you can do is tell me what the fuck is going on."

"I'm going to say this once," Perkins says, getting into my personal space.

His chest is nearly touching mine and I can feel his warm breath on my cheek. My heart is racing, and it takes everything in me to keep my hands at my sides instead of grabbing him, pinning him to the car, and kissing him senseless.

"Fuck off." Perkins's tone is low and dangerous. "If you know what's good for you, stay the fuck out of my life."

"Done."

I take a step back and pull his key fob out of my pocket. His eyes widen when I toss them to him. Before he can say anything, I'm starting the hour-and-a-half run back to campus.

Chapter 6

West

I spend Sundays at breakfast with my mother. She insists on making the two-hour drive to town every week, as if our calls on Wednesdays aren't enough for her. As much as I love her, I wish she would stop coming. She always sits across from me at the diner and tries to pick apart my life, as if what I'm doing isn't enough for her.

Then there are the comparisons she likes to make when it comes to me and my siblings. Both of them have already graduated from college and are building careers for themselves, working on starting families, and settling into their lives.

Meanwhile, my mom likes to think I'm just wandering around aimlessly in life without any ambition. She has never believed I could make a career out of football, and she's never bothered to try to understand it.

Neither has my father, although he doesn't sit across from me once a week and try to pick me apart.

I sigh as I look in the mirror, gripping the edge of the sink. The dark circles beneath my eyes haven't disappeared in the few days since I was at the clinic. My cheeks look hollow and my skin is about three shades paler than it should be.

There's no way she's going to think everything is going well when I look like shit.

I need Mom to believe I'm fine. If she thinks anything is wrong, she'll start hovering. She's always been overbearing, especially when she thinks I'm sick. The last time I had the flu, she barely left my bedside.

Thomas and Laurie never had to put up with her hovering. They both like to say it's because I'm the baby of the family. As the youngest, I'm the one she worries about the most.

I think they're both full of shit.

With another sigh, I run my hand through my hair. The guilt is eating away at me and has been since Shane left me in the parking lot. I had been an ass to him; I know that. I'm still not sure why I care so much, but there was something in the look he gave me. It ripped me in half. I had hurt him, yet again, when all he had done was help me.

Leaving my haunted reflection, I head to the student parking lot to get in my car. It takes me a few moments to start the engine, but once I do, I nearly switch it back off.

Shane is standing at the other end of the parking lot, his head tipped back as he laughs. My eyes trace the long line of his throat and the way his shirt tightens over his chest as he grabs a box from the girl he's with.

Shaking my head, I pull out of the parking space and turn up the music. Thinking about the way Shane looks is not normal for me. He's attractive enough, from a purely objective angle, but he isn't my type. Women are my type.

Drumming my fingers on the wheel to the beat of the music, I leave campus far behind and head toward town. Mom will be waiting, no matter how early I arrive. She always is. That's why I stop at a coffee shop on the way, suspecting I'll need all the caffeine I can get before I see her.

I sip the coffee as I drive, dread starting to curl in the pit of my stomach. I love my mom, I really do, but she can be a little too much sometimes. Each week is like a brand-new investigation that has been launched into my life.

When I arrive at the café, Mom is already sitting at a table outside. I finish the last of my coffee and throw the cup out before joining her. She looks at me, her eyes moving slowly over my face before traveling down the rest of my body.

I consider turning around and heading back to my car. I don't want to know what she's seeing when she looks at me. For all I know, she's already making a list of all the things she needs to change about me.

Either that or a list of ways I could be more like Thomas and Laurie.

"Weston," Mom says, standing up to pull me into a tight hug. "You're early for once."

"Mom," I say, rolling my eyes as I step back and sit down in my seat. "I'm early every week."

She laughs and shakes her head, sitting down and sipping from her glass of water. Her hair, the same shade as mine, falls in waves over her shoulders, catching the sun overhead and shining brightly. Mom looks at me over the edge of her glass, crossing her eyes to draw a smile out of me.

"There you are," she says as she sets her glass down. "How are you doing? You look a little tired."

"I *am* a little tired. The closer I get to graduation, the more nervous I am. I still don't know what I'm supposed to do after I graduate next year."

"Weston, you're only twenty. Nobody is expecting you to have your entire life figured out yet."

"Sure feels that way," I say, tracing a finger through the condensation on my own water. "Scouts are starting to watch me. Coach told me they'd be in the stands, and I seem to be paying more attention to them than to the game. I don't think I'm playing as well as I used to, since I know they're sitting there."

Mom's eyebrows pull together. "Is football what's making you so tired? It seems like a lot to worry about. Are you sure you don't have too much on your plate? Thomas and

Laurie never had as much going on as you do. Maybe you should talk to one of them about what their extracurriculars looked like. Football might not be the best option while you're trying to focus on getting a degree."

I don't bother to argue with her about that. No matter how many times I have tried to tell her that football is more than just an extracurricular activity for me, she doesn't listen. I can't see the point in wasting my breath any more than I already have.

A waitress appears and sets down menus in front of us. She takes our drink orders before walking away. I watch her for a moment, noticing the way her jeans cling to her gorgeous ass and toned legs. If I wanted to, I could follow her and get her number. A few months ago, I would have.

I don't know what keeps me from getting up now and following the pretty brunette.

"She's gorgeous," Mom says, nodding after the server. "Have you found yourself a nice girlfriend yet? You know, your father and I met when we were at college. We had a bunch of the same classes and he used to sit beside me in every one of them until he worked up the nerve to talk to me."

"I know. You tell me all the time."

Mom grins and nods. "Maybe if you found a nice girlfriend, you wouldn't spend as much time wearing yourself out on the football field. You know I worry a lot that you're going to get hurt. What happens if you get hurt?"

"I'll be fine, Mom. I've been playing for years and nothing bad has happened yet. You need to stop worrying about me."

"What about your grades, Weston?" she asks, not acknowledging anything I've said. "You know, your grades usually start to slip when you are this focused on football."

"Mom, I'm okay. Alright? My GPA hasn't started slipping. I'm balancing school and football as much as I can without running myself into the ground."

We pause our conversation when the server comes back with our drinks and takes our food order. Mom smiles until the server is gone before she frowns at me and shakes her head.

"Weston, I think all this football is a bad idea. Look at how tired it's making you! You know, being this exhausted isn't good for you."

I sigh and run a hand through my hair. "Why won't you listen to me? I'm doing fine. I'm playing the sport I love. My GPA is good. I'm excelling in my classes. I'm doing everything I'm supposed to do, but it's still not good enough for you."

"Weston, enough. I didn't say that and quite frankly, the way you're acting is making you seem childish. All I said is that you can't be this tired. It isn't good for you. The exhaustion will wear you down until you're sick and it compromises your immune system. Then what happens?"

I shrug and sip my drink. "I don't know what happens after that, but I'm not going to stop living my life just because you hate the fact that I play football. Why can't you just be proud of all I'm accomplishing?"

Mom's face flushes a bright red and her nails dig into her palms. "When have I ever said I'm not proud of you? I just wish you had chosen a more traditional path like Laurie and Thomas did."

And yet another comparison to my siblings.

"You're making it pretty clear by the way you're talking about football as if it's just something that shouldn't matter to me. I'm one of the best tight ends in the state. I'm being scouted by the NFL. Mom, I have a chance to make something of myself."

"You have a chance of making something of yourself no matter what you choose to do with your life. You are a bright and capable young man, but I don't think football is a good use of your time. Football players are lucky if they make it to thirty. Then what happens?"

"I don't know, Mom. You just said a few minutes ago I don't have to have it all figured out right now. You said it's okay and now you're telling me it's only okay as long as I give up on football. I'm going to have a college degree in economics in a little less than two years. That seems like something I could fall back on, don't you think?"

I run a hand through my hair, my heart hammering in my chest. Mom has never liked the fact that I play football. Over the last several years, she has tried dozens of times to pull me out of the sport and steer me in a more academic direction. After all, she and my dad are both academics. Why wouldn't I want to be just like them? And then there's my doctor brother and lawyer sister. Any of the other options would be better in her mind. Hell, I'm sure she'd be happy to see me bagging groceries for a living — not that I'm belittling those who do — as long as I'm not playing football.

If I had the time, I could think of dozens of reasons why I want something different for myself.

I do well in my classes, but I don't want to make a career out of being an academic. I want to play football until I can't anymore and then after that, I can figure out what else to do. Right now, football is the future I always hoped I could have.

"Weston, you can do anything you want, but I don't see why what you want is to chase a ball up and down a field with a bunch of other sweaty men who barely know how to spell."

I freeze, anger coursing through me. All through high school and the first two years of college, people have labeled me as a stupid football player, a dumb jock. People think that because I play a sport, I'm not smart.

It hurts to hear my mom repeat the same thing I've heard at least once a week over the course of the last six years.

"Wow," I say, taking a deep breath and trying to smother my anger, my disappointment. "Okay. I think we need to get something clear. I don't know what I want when I reach fifty, but I know right now, I want to play football. As for the players who can barely spell, most of the team have GPAs close to or even higher than mine. Only two don't and that's because their major is engineering and the program is about a thousand times harder."

Mom offers me an apologetic look. "I didn't mean it the way it came out."

"I'm done talking about it," I say, clenching my glass of water. "If you bring it up again, I'm going back to campus. Your stupid jock of a son has several tests to study for."

Mom's lips curl downward as the food is placed in front of us. We fall into a conversation, keeping the topics safe. She goes on and on, barely pausing for a breath as I pick at my food. My stomach is tossing and turning, my mind anywhere but on breakfast.

When I get back to campus, I will have to study. Part of me thinks I should find Shane and apologize, but the other part isn't sure it's a good idea. Shane made it clear he's done with me. Maybe the best thing I can do for both of us is to respect that.

I finish my breakfast, wondering why my mind is so messed up when it comes to him. I could understand it if he were a friend going through hard times, but I barely know him. He's nothing in my life. And yet, I still can't shake the guilt that lingers.

When mom and I are done with breakfast, I pay the bill and say goodbye before heading to my car. As I drive back to campus, I keep the music up loud, trying to numb my mind.

Chapter 7

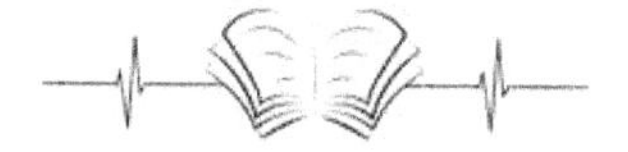

Shane

I don't know why I followed Perkins here. Being at a party is still a bad idea for me, yet I followed him down to one, knowing it would likely get me in trouble.

When he came back to the dorm earlier, he didn't look good. I could hear some of the students whispering about a game the football team had lost earlier that evening. They're still whispering about it now, though fewer of them seem to care as they fill red solo cups with amber liquid.

"What are you doing here?" Ethan asks, appearing beside me with a bottle of water. "I thought you were strongly against parties?"

"I'm not against them," I say, nearly shouting to be heard above the pounding bass guitarist of Liquid Flames. The bassist moves across a makeshift stage, grinning as the lead guitarist rolls his eyes and turns his back on him.

"Oh? I thought you were, since I've only seen you at one."

"You don't go to that many either," I say, walking to a cooler on the other side of the room and pulling out my own bottle of water. "Most weekends you're holed up in the library."

"Things change," he says with a shrug, his eyes drifting over the crowd until he locks onto somebody on the other side of the room. "I've got to go before that idiot makes a giant mistake."

"Idiot?" My eyebrows furrow as I try to see who he was looking at. Ethan says nothing, and in a matter of seconds, he disappears into the crowd.

I scan the room, trying to see past the writhing bodies and couples lurking in dark corners. Perkins is nowhere to be seen, but many of his teammates are playing beer pong while girls drape themselves over them.

Is Perkins with a girl somewhere? My stomach twists with jealousy, dropping down to my feet. *Not your problem. You know better than to go chasing after a straight man, anyway.*

"Great," I mutter, opening my bottle of water and drinking half. Just perfect. I'm stupid. I need to go back to my dorm and study instead of loitering around a party I have no business being at.

I move through the mass of people, still searching for Perkins. When I find him, he's leaning beside one of the kegs and sipping from a cup. He tosses his head back as he laughs at something the pretty blonde beside him says. My heart skips a beat as I try to memorize the smile on his face before it disappears again.

As I push my traitorous heart to the side, I wander closer to him. The girl winks at him before walking away and I seize my chance to get closer to him. Perkins looks at me, the smile disappearing and a frown taking its place.

"Are you sure drinking while you're on a ton of medication is a good idea?"

Perkins's face pales, his eyes narrowing. "First of all, fuck you. Second, it's root beer."

Perkins shoves off the wall he's leaning on and walks away, shaking his head. Even though he says he isn't drinking, I don't miss the stumble in his step as he weaves through the gyrating bodies of the students dancing. He is unsteady on his feet at best. To the other partygoers, it would look like he's drunk. For a moment, I wonder if the stumble is on purpose or if there is something wrong.

After everything else I've seen of him, I don't want to leave what happens next up to chance. It's possible Perkins could pass out or start coughing up blood again. My chest tightens as I look around for him, waiting to see if he reappears. When he doesn't, I pull out my phone and glance at the time.

It's getting late and I shouldn't be here, but I can't leave him to fend for himself.

With a sigh, I finish my water and toss the bottle into a trash can before heading in the direction Perkins disappeared. I walk through the halls of the frat house, looking for any sign of the football players. Where one goes, the rest usually follow.

When I hear chanting, I know they're near. I enter the backyard, glancing at several kegs all in a row. Football players are upside down, doing keg stands as they drink cheap beer as fast as possible.

"Great," I say under my breath, looking around for Perkins.

Lights are strung through the trees, and more lights line the backyard. There's a small fire going in the pit — a pit I'm sure they aren't allowed to have — and a pile of fireworks in one corner.

Perkins is sitting on a bench in the far corner, leaning back against the fence. He's slumped in on himself, his chest rising and falling rapidly. As I approach him, he closes his eyes and sighs.

"Shane! Over here!" Ethan yells.

I look to the right and see Ethan standing with a few other guys. Several of them are attractive and it has been months since I was last with somebody. I could walk away from Perkins now and try my luck with someone who might actually be interested in me.

"Later!" I grin before turning to Perkins.

He's standing now and stumbling toward the pool. Lurching from side to side as he walks, it looks like it's only a matter of time before he falls headfirst into the cool depths of the water.

I move quickly, crossing the yard to stand beside him. Perkins looks over at me, a frown on his face. He opens his mouth to say something, but he shakes his head and turns to the pool.

"Want to go swimming?" Perkins asks, pointing down at the water. "Looks like it would be a good swim. We could do that."

"We are not swimming." I shake my head. "You might not be drunk, but something is wrong with you."

"Nothing's wrong with me." His words slur together. "I'm fine. You're the one that's not fine. You always have this wrinkle in your forehead, like something is really bothering you."

The world around us comes to a screeching halt as he steps up to me and smooths a finger over my forehead. His touch sends electric shocks through my body, straight to my cock. I clear my throat and take a step back, knowing if he were in his right mind, he wouldn't be this close to me, and he certainly wouldn't be touching me.

"How about I take you back to your dorm and you can sleep whatever this is off?" I cajole. "Come on, let's go."

"I don't want to."

I sigh and step closer to him. He stands taller than me, and he has several more pounds of muscle. And I imagine myself wrapped in his arms, but only for a moment.

Perkins frowns as he looks down at me. "What?" His chest is still rising and falling rapidly.

"Get your ass moving, now. I'm getting tired of playing your damn white knight," I say, my tone low as I point toward the driveway.

"Fine," he mutters, looking like a scolded child.

***

We've only just reached his door when Perkins gags, his hand clamping over his mouth. He digs the keys out of his pocket and hurries to open the door before hurrying to the bathroom. The door slams behind him and moments later, I hear the sound of retching.

I should leave and let him be sick in peace, but my stupid attraction to him keeps me rooted in place. With a sigh, I walk around the room, looking at the books on his shelves.

Several of the books were ones that my teachers had assigned me to read in high school, and others I read with my mom. If Perkins kept them, he must like them. I'm surprised to see we have similar tastes.

My fingers run over the spines of the books as I make my way around the room. I stop at the last bookshelf and I'm delighted to see the book I'm currently reading on my tablet. Since I have nothing else to do while waiting to see if I'll have to take Perkins to the hospital or not, I settle down on the floor with the book.

I don't know how long it is before the door to the bathroom opens and Perkins stumbles out, looking more alert than he did before.

"What are you doing here?" Perkins asks, confusion crossing his face when he sees me sitting with the book in my hand. "I didn't ask you to come here." His eyes flit over to the book I have in my hand. "And what the hell are you reading?"

"First of all, fuck you," I said, repeating the exact words he said to me earlier. "Second, the person, be it gentleman — *which you obviously are not* — or lady who has not pleasure in a good novel, must be intolerably stupid." I rise to my feet and return the book to the shelf.

He quirks a brow. "Jane Austen's *Northanger Abbey*, huh?" For a brief moment, his eyes gleam in amusement, before his barriers lock back in place.

Ignoring both his comment — although it's hot that he knows one of Austen's famous quotes, which has effectively made my dick harden — and the way my fingers ache with the need to touch him, I say, "I stayed to make sure you didn't kill yourself while throwing up. Now that you're fine, I'll be going."

I make my way to the door but stop when a hand wraps around my wrist and pulls me back. The stupid tingling happens again as I turn around and face him, yanking my wrist out of his grip.

"What do you want?" I hate the sound of desperation in my voice. "I don't know what's wrong with you, Perkins, but I know something is. Stop acting like an asshole for once in your life."

"I'm sorry." He looks down at the floor.

"Well, you should be." I yank the door open, looking at Perkins over my shoulder. "If you're ever ready to stop acting like a prick, let me know. Whatever you're going through, I figure you could probably use a friend."

He says nothing as I walk away.

I head down the hall and back to my own room, knowing that as much as I may be attracted to him, he's never going to change.

Chapter 8

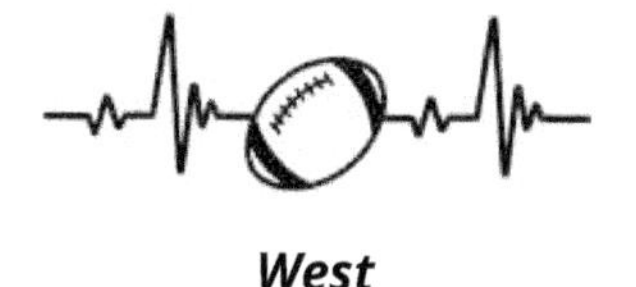

West

All I could think about in the past week is Shane. I could see the hurt on his face when he walked out of my room that night, but I didn't know what to do. The feelings I have for him are confusing and complicated. I've only ever been attracted to women before, but he makes me curious. He makes me want to try things I've never even considered before.

It scares the living shit out of me.

With everything else happening in my life, I don't have time to deal with these feelings. I don't want to figure out whether I'm attracted to him or whether the medications I'm taking are playing with my mind.

I sigh as I get out of bed and head to the bathroom. I turn on the water and strip down, running a hand down my face. The water is scalding against my skin, sending a shock through my system and loosening the tight muscles in my back. Practice this morning was brutal.

When I step out of the shower, the nerves are tearing through my body in full swing. I have taken several blood tests since the last time I saw the doctor. This appointment was to confirm what I suspected was already happening.

I don't want to go alone, but there's no way I'm going to ask Mom to come with me. She'll spend most of the time panicking. Dad will just be closed off, tension simmering just beneath the surface; sounds familiar, right? Bottom line is, I need somebody whose presence will calm me, keep me grounded.

Neither of my parents is that person.

I could ask one of the guys from the team — Anderson or Maddox maybe — but that would mean the rest of my teammates would know. They would tell the coach and I might lose everything I've been working for.

Everything I've dedicated my life to thus far would slip away. Scouts would stop looking for me at the games. Coach Veer would take me off the team. He would never forgive me for hiding something this big from him.

I stare at the bottles of medication that line one of my bookshelves. Shane has seen them. It bothers me that I don't know whether he knows my secret or not. He hasn't said that he does. In fact, he tells me he still doesn't. If he's telling the truth, it means he isn't searching for whatever is wrong with me.

When I was younger, I never thought anything like this would happen to me. I didn't think every Friday morning I'd be driving to the nearest town and talking with a doctor about my health. I didn't think that I would be sneaking around without telling my friends what was going on.

Yet here I am.

Without my mom and my friends, that leaves me with one option.

After I get dressed, I head down the hall to Shane's room. I can hear music playing on the other side of the door. Much of his schedule matches mine, leaving his Friday mornings wide open. Yes, I've been noticing him more and more lately. Don't ask me why.

I raise my fist to knock on the door and consider what will happen. He could laugh in my face and tell me to get lost. After the way I've treated him, I wouldn't blame him at all. I've been awful and I wish I had a good reason for it.

With a sigh, I knock loudly. My heart is racing, and my head is spinning. I shouldn't be here. I'm an adult. I could go to my appointment on my own without anyone, without *him*.

As I'm turning away to do just that, the door opens, and Shane appears. He looks as if he's only woken up recently, his jeans slung low around his hips and a shirt tossed over his shoulder. My eyes trail along the finely sculpted muscles of his chest, his toned stomach, and his happy trail that leads to... Goddammit. My cheeks are ablaze, and I look away. What the fuck is wrong with me? I shouldn't be looking at Shane in that way.

"What do you want?" His voice is cold as he leans against the doorframe and crosses his arms. "I don't have time to play games with you, Perkins. I don't want to keep doing this."

"I know. I'm sorry. I just...I have an appointment today and it's a big one. I can't ask anyone else to go with me because they don't know anything's wrong, but your nosy ass has gotten involved."

"Why would I go with you?"

I shrug. "I don't know. Sorry." Turning away from him, I brace myself to head to my car alone.

"Perkins," he mutters before sighing. "I'll go with you on one condition."

Turning back around, I look at him. "Really?"

Shane looks at me for a moment before smirking. "Say it."

"Say what?" I ask, feigning ignorance.

"Say you need my help and then I'll go with you."

"Do I really have to?"

Shane rolls his eyes and shakes his head. "No, I'm not an asshole. Give me a minute to finish getting dressed."

"Alright."

Shane leaves the door wide open as he steps back into his dorm to get dressed. The small room is cramped with both his belongings and his roommate's. I step inside and take a look around. One side of the room is more organized than the other, as if the person living on that side can't stand a little mess.

Shane heads to the clean side and pulls on his shirt before rummaging in a drawer for a pair of socks. Once he's dressed, he grabs his keys and wallet, stuffing them into his pocket. He slides on a jacket and looks down at his phone.

"Is this going to take a long time? I have some studying I need to do this afternoon," Shane says as he brushes by me.

His arm touches my torso when he moves and everything inside me feels as if it's on fire. Shane's eyes flicker up to mine, something lingering there before he looks away and keeps walking. At that moment, I know there's something between us that I can't keep ignoring.

I don't have time to figure it out either.

I follow him out of the dorm and to the student parking lot. Before I start the car, I gesture toward the book displayed on Shane's phone.

"Tell me."

Shane fixes his eyes on me, as if trying to figure me out. Then he does it, one of the few times he has done it in my presence; he smiles at me, a smile that slowly builds. It makes him even more attractive and hot and all the good things. Yes, I'm finally admitting it to myself, Shane is fucking hot.

I quirk a brow at him. "Well?"

"'We must take the good wherever we find it and try to remove the bad wherever it may be.' It's from a collection of letters Indira Gandhi's father wrote to her."

"I've heard of her."

"My mom was a history and literature buff, and got me interested in reading beyond our required readings in high school. My minor is literature, so it keeps me on my toes, and I'm making my way through what many deem as classic literature."

Shane's passion enthralls me. I can see how deeply engrossed he gets when he's reading. His eyes light up. It's obvious he isn't reading for reading's sake, so it's no surprise literature is his minor — he probably should have majored in it. Who knows? The point is, he simply, irrevocably loves to read.

"Your mom was?"

Shane's eyes become sober, losing their shine. "She died less than a year ago."

"I'm sorry."

"Thank you," he says simply.

Pressing the engine start button, the car rumbles to life. The drive is quiet. Shane continues to read while I listen to music.

When we park outside the clinic, Shane is quick to get out. He walks to the door and yanks it open, waiting for me. I follow him inside and stop at the counter to check in with the receptionist.

"Hello, Weston." Nurse Ricki smiles as she hands me my health card. "Have a seat and Dr. Sullivan will be with you in a few minutes."

Shane is already sitting and reading and when I sit down beside him, the silence between us is tense. This is unfamiliar territory, a strange friendship we have going on. Neither of us knows what we're supposed to be doing.

"Well, this is fun, Weston," Shane says, smirking as I shake my head.

"I hate being called Weston. Weston Perkins the Third. My parents couldn't have given me a more pretentious name if they tried."

Shane laughs, and the sound makes my heart race. I scowl and look down at my hands, trying to distract myself.

"Is this going to be bad?" He tucks his phone into his pocket. "You look like you think it's going to be bad."

"I don't think it's going to be good," I counter, closing my eyes and leaning the back of my head against the wall. "You can leave if you want."

"No. I said I'd be here if you wanted help. I'm here."

We fall into another silence that is slightly more comfortable until Nurse Ricki calls my name. I stand and take a deep breath, stuffing my hands into my pockets to hide the shaking. I don't need Shane to see how nervous I really am.

Dr. Sullivan is sitting behind her desk with a thick file in front of her when I walk into her office. There is a sympathetic smile on her face and I already have an idea of what is coming before she opens her mouth. Over the last few years, I've started to notice the way doctors look at me when they're about to give me bad news.

"Hello, Weston," Dr. Sullivan says softly, opening the file as I take a seat. "How have you been feeling lately?"

"Not great. I coughed up some blood. I feel sick all the time and I'm exhausted."

"Well, I'm afraid all of that is pretty standard. I know you asked me to run a few tests the last time you were in."

I nod. "Yeah, it feels like something is changing."

"Your juvenile hemochromatosis is getting worse," Dr. Sullivan says, not bothering to soften her words. I've always told her to never mince words with me, just shoot straight. And look how I'm thinking about idioms and shit. I should tell Shane I'm being smart and literary, just like him.

The doctor clears her throat, which jolts me out of my musings. "What is happening right now is that your liver is failing."

The air is knocked out of my lungs as I look at her and take a deep breath. I want to start screaming. I want to run from the room and tell everyone who will listen that it isn't fair.

I've been taking my meds and coming to every doctor's visit. I've been doing everything right. I follow all the instructions from the doctors and stay as healthy as possible, even with the disease.

"How bad is the liver failure?" I ask after a moment. My voice is shaky, and I know I'm on the verge of breaking down. None of this is how my life is supposed to be.

"Based on the blood tests and the imaging we did, we can confirm you are in early-stage liver failure."

"So, I'm going to die." I run my hands through my hair.

This isn't fair. None of this is fair. I'm too young to die. I have too many things I want to do with my life. I can't die yet.

"If we don't get you a new liver quickly, then yes."

I inhale and exhale slowly, gripping the arms of the chair to stop my hands from shaking. "And how do we start getting me a new liver? Will that even help anything? I was told there's no cure for the disease."

"A new liver will sustain your life, but you will still be on medication for the rest of your life to manage the disease."

"Either way, I'm fucked."

She smiles softly. "In the simplest terms, yes. But you are young and otherwise healthy. I've put you on the transplant list and gotten in touch with a specialist. As soon as a liver that matches becomes available, it's yours."

"And if one doesn't magically appear, I'm dead."

"Weston, there's still time. The specialist and I have a treatment plan in place. Dialysis will help in the meantime, but you'll have to go to the hospital several times a week for it. Listen, I know this is a lot to take in, especially for someone so young. Do you have anyone with you today that you want to be in here while we talk about where we go from here?"

For a moment I picture how much Shane being by my side would help me to get through this, but I quickly dismiss it and steel myself to face this crisis. I look back up at the doctor and shake my head. "No."

"Alright." Her eyes search mine. "Let's talk about your next steps, then."

***

After an hour with Dr. Sullivan, I walk back out to the waiting room. Shane is still slumped in his chair and on his phone, probably reading. My stomach lurches and my heart pounds as I see him still waiting there. I don't know what to make of that.

"I thought you would have been gone by now," I say, intentionally snapping at him. "I don't want you here anymore. Once we get back to campus, let's just pretend this never happened."

Shane gets up and tucks his phone into his pocket. "You look like you just got the worst news of your life. What kind of person would I be if I believe you right now? Act like an ass all you want. I'm not going anywhere."

"Well, you should. This isn't your problem to deal with."

Even I can hear the barely-held-back tears struggling to break free. I swallow hard and head to the door, not bothering to see if he is following me. Shane sighs from somewhere behind me and seconds later the car keys are being ripped from my hand.

"Give me back my fucking keys," I say, getting into his face. Our chests are nearly touching and my heart is racing. I have no clue what I'm doing or why, but it feels right. It gives me something to focus on other than my disease.

Shane quirks an eyebrow before stepping around me. "You're not in the right mindset to drive. I have a license and I've driven your car before. Now get in the car and shut up. I'm not dealing with this shit right now."

"Why not?" I ask, goading him into another argument. "You wanted to be the one to involve yourself in my problems, my life. You said you wanted to help, remember? Well, if you want to be involved you get to deal with this side now."

Shane takes a step toward me, his head tilting back to glare up at me. If I lowered my head even slightly, our lips would be pressed together. The thought pisses me off even more.

"Be mad at the entire fucking world for all I care, Perkins. Just do it in the fucking car."

He says nothing else as he takes a step back and gets in the car, slamming the door behind him. My chest is heaving as I walk around the front of the car and get in the passenger side, sinking down into the seat.

I clench my hands into fists, my heart racing. I want to scream. I want to break everything. I'm so fucking frustrated and angry and I have nowhere to channel that energy.

"I don't know what happened in there," Shane says softly as we drive out of the lot and turn onto the highway that leads toward TU. "You don't have to tell me either. What I do know is that pizza and some root beer will fix everything."

I chuckle darkly and shake my head. "I wish that was true."

Shane shrugs and drums his long fingers on the wheel. "True or not, it's better than sitting around by yourself and feeling like shit."

"Alright, fine."

I close my eyes and slump against the window as Shane drives. He doesn't bother me with questions or his sympathy. He doesn't do what everyone else in my life would do. Instead, he leaves me to think things through.

There are no false promises of *it will get better* from him. No fake hope that everything will be alright.

Somehow, I know if I tell him what's going on, there would be no pitying looks from him. None. At. All. And it's refreshing.

***

When we get back to the dorm, Shane orders a pizza on his phone while I lead the way up to my dorm. He follows me inside and takes a seat on the desk chair, kicking off his shoes and resting his feet on the edge of my bed. "You don't mind, do you?"

"No, I don't."

I flop down into the bed and turn on the television. Shane says nothing as I flip to a football game and turn up the sound. Neither of us moves or says anything until the pizza and soda are delivered. Even then, we are too busy eating to say much.

As we watch the football game, Shane's eyes are glued to the screen. I don't know how much of it he understands. I've never seen him at any of my games and

I doubt I ever will. Seeing him sitting on my floor and reading a book the other day seems much more his style.

"You haven't asked what's wrong with me," I say eventually, after sneaking several glances at him.

"Didn't think it was any of my business. If you wanted me to know, you would have told me by now." He looks at me for a second, shrugs, and turns his attention back to the game.

"Do you go to any of the games?" I ask, trying to get him to talk to me.

"Nope."

I run a hand through my hair. "Do you want to? You could come hang out with the team after."

I don't know why I asked him to come to a game. I don't know why it seemed as if those words carried the weight of the world. It feels like I am asking a girl to wear my jersey and watch me play like I used to in high school.

All of this is too much. Too complicated. I should tell him I'm only joking.

Shane studies me for a moment, a strange expression on his face before he nods. "Alright, I'll come to the next game."

My heart plummets to my feet as panic surges through my body. I didn't think this through at all.

Chapter 9

Shane

I don't know what I'm doing at a football game. I don't even like football. Hell, the only part of the game I enjoy is seeing the players in their tight pants. Same thing goes for baseball. Beyond that, it's just a bunch of sweaty jocks flinging their bodies at each other while they chase a ball around the field.

At least, that's what I had thought until I watched Perkins play.

Even before the game started, there was an intensity to him that I hadn't seen before. He leaned into the huddle before the game, nodding along with what the other players were saying.

A cold breeze blows through the stands, sending me shivering deeper into the leather jacket I'm wearing. I put more effort into my appearance before the game than I would have normally. I want Perkins to notice me and start seeing me as something more than that annoying guy who lives down the hall.

That is a problem of its own. As far as I know, he's straight, like an arrow straight, and my crush on him is causing more and more issues. I spend too much time looking at and thinking about him. Sooner or later, he's bound to find out.

I need to get laid and get over him.

No good ever comes from being attracted to a straight man.

The referee blows the whistle and the players head to the sidelines as the cheerleaders take to the field. People are cheering and laughing as the cheerleaders do their routine. The football players have their helmets ripped off and are downing water or pointing to the scoreboard as they talk. I don't know what's happening, but I do know we're in the lead.

Perkins stands in the middle of the players, talking to Ethan's friend Maddox. Perkins laughs at something Maddox says before looking around the stands. His eyes lock with mine and he gives a sharp nod before turning back to the team.

Another whistle is blown a few minutes later, and the players head back onto the field. I watch as they run out and get into position again. Perkins shifts his weight from side to side before going still as the ball goes flying.

The next thing I know, Perkins is being taken to the ground. The sound of plastic shoulder pads slamming against each other is loud. Nobody seems to notice. They all keep running with the ball, getting closer and closer to the end zone.

A few seconds after getting hit, Perkins is back on his feet and running again. He moves through the other players easily. There's something about the way he moves that makes him stand out from all the others. He seems like he's a natural at this, as if he was born to play.

Whatever's wrong with him, I hope it doesn't stop him from playing.

When the game ends, I get a text from him telling me where the team is heading and to meet him by his car. I sigh and run a hand through my hair. I should leave. I have several tests coming up and I need to study for them. Going to a party just to spend time with a guy who doesn't like me is a bad idea.

As I leave the stands, I catch sight of my uncle waiting in the parking lot. He looks around, frowning when our eyes meet. Uncle James nods at me before jerking his head to the side.

I follow him beneath the stands, knowing that nobody will see us here. If the other students know he's my uncle, it will only cause more problems for me.

"What do you think you're doing?" Uncle James asks, crossing his arms over his chest. "I thought I told you to stay out of trouble, but I'm getting reports from the professors that you've missed some of their classes recently."

"My friend hasn't been doing well and needed someone around."

Uncle James pinches the bridge of his nose. "Look, I can understand you want to help people. That's your mother's soft-hearted nature in you. It's not always a great thing. You're putting your own future at risk because of it. There's nothing else I can do to defend you if you mess this up, Shane."

"You don't have to keep telling me that." I wish I was anywhere but here. "I know I shouldn't have missed class, but my friend needed someone and I'm not going to be the person who leaves them there to suffer alone."

"I can appreciate that, but I don't think you're telling me the truth. One of the professors said they saw you leaving a party two weeks ago. That's not how you keep yourself out of trouble, Shane. Why are you so determined to ruin your future?"

"I'm not!" My voice is sharp, sharper than I intended. "Why do you think the worst of me all the time? I'm working hard. I'm getting good grades. I had a good reason to miss class."

"I don't care what your reasons were." My uncle shakes his head. "Don't be any more of a disappointment to your mother, Shane. I can't keep protecting you."

His words are like a sharp knife plunging straight into my chest. He knows the weight of his words. I can tell he does from the glint in his eye. Uncle James has never been a kind man, but I thought our relationship would improve if I went to the school he was the dean of.

Clearly, I'm wrong. Our relationship is never going to be good and I might as well stop hoping for anything different.

"You're the only disappointment to the family," I say before turning and heading to the parking lot.

Perkins is standing outside his car with his gym bag on the ground beside him when I approach. He slings his arm over my shoulder, steering me toward the concession stand as his stomach growls. Fire travels through my body at the innocent touch, and I fight the urge to jerk away from him.

"Come on, I'm hungry," he says with a grin and another audible growl of his stomach.

Thankfully, he drops his arm before I can turn to him and blurt out how he makes me feel, how I feel about him. I'm quiet as he orders his food, refusing his offer to buy me something to eat, not wanting to risk opening my mouth and allowing word vomit to spill from my lips.

"Are you alright?" he asks, his attitude surprisingly caring.

"Fine. Just dealing with some family stuff."

Perkins's eyes appraise me as if he doesn't quite believe what I said. "Alright. If you say so."

"I do."

He nods and nearly inhales both of the hot dogs he ordered. When he's done, we get in his car and he drives us back to the dorm. Perkins leaves his gym bag in the car, insisting that he'll deal with it later, although I doubt that. I knew some high school football players who wouldn't wash their uniforms all season because they thought it would bring them good luck.

"I'm going to shower and then you want to meet up at my room before we head to the party?" he asks as we reach our floor.

"Oh, it's a party?"

"Well, we did win. So, there is usually a party. To be honest, there's usually a party if we lose too. The parties for wins are much better, though."

I shake my head. "No thanks. Look, the game was fun, but I'm not in the mood for a party. I have to study."

"Are you sure? I thought you wanted to come."

"Not if it's a party, but thanks. I have a ton of studying to do and it's not going to get done if I go."

My excuse is weak, but it's better than nothing. If he knew the truth about why I can't go to parties — why I really need to stay away from trouble now — he might start seeing me differently.

"Alright." He pulls out his phone to send someone a message. "I'm going to take a shower. Give me like twenty minutes, then come back here with your books and we'll study."

I don't know what to say. On the one hand, I want to tell him I can study alone and don't need him around. He would go to his party and we would both continue going about our lives as if nothing had changed. On the other hand, I want to be with him, desperately.

My desire ultimately wins out and I agree, heading back to my room to gather my books. Needing to study isn't a complete lie; I have multiple tests coming up and half a dozen assignments I need to finish.

When I head back to Perkins's room, there is a pile of takeout containers on his desk with steam rising from them. His textbooks are spread out over the floor with notes among them. I sit on a free spot on the floor and spread out my own books, mentally bracing myself for a long night of studying.

"Help yourself to the food," Perkins says, sitting down beside me. His arm brushes against mine as he reaches across me for a book, and I can hear the beat of my heart and feel it racing.

"Thanks," I say, grabbing a notebook and opening it to a blank page. "You know, you don't have to study with me. You could go out and party with your friends."

"I'd rather be here," he says, glancing at me from the corner of his eyes. "Besides, partying isn't as much fun when you can't drink. Especially if people start to notice you're the only one not drinking."

"I don't know why you would care about what those other people think."

"I don't. It's just easier when I don't have to deal with the strange looks."

I nod and start flipping through my notebook with a highlighter in hand, making more notes of anything relevant on the blank page. Perkins shifts beside me, his leg pressing against mine. I wait for the moment when he notices how close he's sitting and pulls away, but it never comes.

The hair on the back of my neck is standing, and my palms are sweaty. We are close. Too close. Everything about this situation is far too close to my liking. I don't know what's happening, and it scares the living shit out of me.

"Shane, are you okay? You look like you're freaking the fuck out."

"Only a little," I say, trying to brush it off as nothing with a shrug. "These tests are pretty important. I need to get some good grades, otherwise, the professors are going to be more up my ass than they already are."

Perkins rolls his eyes. "I don't get that. The professors don't care. Why would they be more up your ass than anyone else's?"

I swallow hard and shrug again. "Don't know."

He turns and faces me, the scent of his spiced body wash wafting seductively in the air. The scent is intoxicating, drawing me closer until we're inches apart.

"I don't believe you," he says quietly as I glance down at his mouth. "You're hiding something just as much as I am."

I pull back from him, knowing if I got any closer, I would make a mistake that both of us would regret. He clears his throat and turns away from me, grabbing a textbook and opening it up in his lap.

For the rest of the night, we sit in near silence. The tension flows back and forth between us, but neither of us is willing to break it. By the time I decide to head back to my dorm room, neither of us has said a word.

Perkins is right though. Both of us have secrets we aren't willing to talk about.

CHAPTER 10

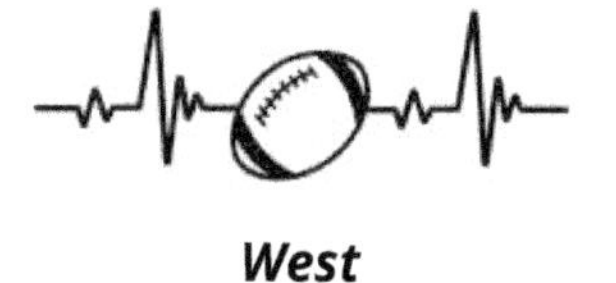

West

I'm reading some of the notes I took in the lecture earlier while trying not to think about the way Shane's compelling eyes keep flickering up to me. It's no secret he's gay; he's never hidden it in the couple of months I've known him. However, it's starting to become more and more obvious he might be attracted to me. His eyes linger when he thinks I'm not looking, and I'd be lying if I said it didn't make me feel a little excited.

I still don't know what to do with that information.

We've been spending more time together lately. When we're in my room, I wish he could, or would stay, and whenever we're in his room, I don't want to leave. He's unlike anyone else I've ever met. He doesn't press me to share my secrets or be anything I'm not. Shane is quiet and steady, but he knows how to have a good time. He's the kind of friend I could have used by my side when I was first diagnosed.

We're in his room now, but I'm still terrified I'm going to end up scaring him away. Who would want to spend time around someone who's terminally ill? Who in their right mind would want to give up their days and nights to sit by my bedside and wait for me to die?

I wouldn't ask him to do that. I couldn't. Even if he was my friend, he doesn't deserve to deal with my issues.

If keeping my secret means he isn't worried about me, I'll keep my secret.

Shane shifts on the bed beside me, taking off his sweater and tossing it across the room. It lands on the chair. He rolls up his sleeves before settling back down to look at his notes. His movement has brought him closer to me. His side is brushing against mine each time he turns the pages in his textbook. He looks at me, licking his bottom lip before reaching for the cup of coffee on the nightstand. To reach it, he has to reach over my back, his arm touching my shoulder blades as he grabs the coffee.

Sparks ignite, even through the layers of my clothes. I freeze, wondering if the medication for my hemochromatosis is playing tricks with my head. I've never been attracted to a man before him — yes, I've said it; I'm attracted to Shane. I've been on more medication than ever lately to try to control my liver failure. It has to be the medication.

"What do you think this means?" Shane asks, setting his coffee back down before pointing to something he had underlined in his notes. "You would think I'd be able to read my own writing, but apparently not."

"Don't know," I say, my voice tight as I look at him. My gaze dips to his mouth, looking at his lips; his thin upper lip is balanced by his plump lower lip, which fucking fascinates me. I imagine those lips on my —

Unknowingly interrupting my NSFW thoughts, Shane says, "Hope it's not important." He shrugs, even while flipping to the page.

Staying here with Shane as it gets later is dangerous. I find myself caring less and less about who I used to be. I want to get to know him better, to find out if he tastes as good as he looks.

Get it together, Perkins.

I shift slightly away from him.

Shane stiffens before his jaw tightens. He flips through some more pages of his notes as my heart beats faster in my chest. Did I insult him? I didn't mean to. I just couldn't deal with all the confusing thoughts right now.

"I should go," I say, climbing off the end of the bed and looking for my shoes. "It's getting late and I have an early practice and then a doctor's appointment."

Shane gets up from his bed and stands in front of me. "Do you need someone to go with you?"

"No." I want him to come with me again, I need him there, but my lips can't form the words to ask him. My chest tightens as his face falls before he nods and turns away.

"Alright. Have a good night."

"Shane." I'm not sure what else I'm going to say, but I can't seem to stand not saying anything. I take a step after him, wanting to reach out. "Will you come with me tomorrow?"

"Look, if you would rather go on your own, that's fine, Perkins. I get it. You don't want to let anybody in to see what you're dealing with."

I sigh and run a hand through my hair. "No. I don't want to go alone, but I might as well. They're running more tests. Nobody will be allowed in the room with me, anyway. That's why I was going to go alone."

And hopefully, those tests show that the dialysis is still working.

Shane turns back to face me, and suddenly we're inches apart. It would be easy to give into the desires that have been running through my mind for the last couple of weeks, but I don't think either of us is ready for that yet. I look down at him, my heart thudding in my chest.

I want to know if what I feel for him is attraction or the medication before I give in to any of the thoughts running wild. I want to know to know for sure I won't hurt him if I cross that line.

I take a step back and stuff my hands into my pockets. It's easier to control myself if there is a barrier in the way, preventing me from touching him.

"Are you okay?"

"Fine, Shane. I'll see you later?"

He nods, his eyes distant as he looks past me at the door. After another awkward moment, I leave, shutting the door on whatever had just been happening between us.

***

Football conditioning has never gotten any easier, no matter how many years I've done it. My body still screams in protest each time I do one push-up too many.

I wasn't lying last night when I told Shane I had football practice early in the morning. While I hoped it would be scrimmages, Coach had other ideas. He's pushing us through an awful weightlifting and cardio session that has me ready to throw up.

"Two more sets!" Coach yells after glancing at the large clock on the wall. "After that, you can hit the showers."

I complete my sets quickly, eager for a shower to wash away the sweat. My shirt and shorts are soaked through and my lungs ache. Coach nods to me as I head into the locker room. He hasn't pulled me aside since the last time we talked in his office.

As the other guys enter the locker room, I start to notice the way their maroon and gold uniforms cling to their bodies. I watch the way their muscles move as they tug off their uniforms and disappear into the showers.

I shake my head, trying to get rid of the thoughts of my teammates naked.

Instead of heading to the showers, I grab my gym bag and leave the locker room. In the weight room, Anderson is still lifting heavy dumbbells, the muscles in his back tightening and showing off his definition. I feel myself growing hard and my cheeks flame as I turn away.

This is the last thing I need right now.

Picturing things that annoy me is a trick I learned in high school, and it usually works. My dick, which was semi-erect in my tight pants, softens before I start thinking with the wrong head.

I leave the gym and head back to my dorm. There is barely enough time to shower and get dressed before I have to leave for the doctor.

Getting into my car, I take a deep breath. My hands are shaking as I grip the wheel, ready to head out.

The passenger side door suddenly opens and Shane slides into the seat, not saying anything as he shuts the door and sips his coffee.

"What are you doing?" I ask, looking at him with wide eyes.

"I'm going to your appointment with you." Shane sets his drink in the cupholder.

"You're going to be sitting in the waiting room for a few hours."

"That's fine."

I hate the feeling of hope that takes up residence in my chest. He isn't going anywhere, even if it does mean spending hours in a hospital with me.

"You're going to be bored out of your mind," I say, trying to do anything I can to get him out of my car before I ruin whatever this strange friendship is.

"That's fine. I have games on my phone and hundreds of books I can choose from."

I sigh and shake my head. "Shane, this is insane."

He shrugs. "You're going to be late for your appointment."

I glance at the clock on the dash and scowl. He's right. If I wait another five minutes to leave, I will be late for the appointment. The specialist, Dr. Hartford, and Dr. Sullivan would not be happy with me if I show up late to another appointment. They've already had to wait for me twice and Dr. Sullivan made it clear she would call Coach if I didn't get my act together.

For now, I'm still allowed to play football, even if my liver is failing. I don't want to do anything to put that at risk.

"It's going to be a long time and you're missing classes. I thought you said you couldn't afford to get into any more trouble," I say as one last attempt to get him to leave. The excuse sounds weak to me too, and I know he isn't going to take the bait.

Shane rolls his eyes and leans back in his seat, stretching his legs in front of him, before crossing them at the ankles. He looks comfortable as he settles in, clearly not going anywhere.

"Perkins, there are some things in life worth getting into trouble for."

Chapter 11

Shane

As I look at Perkins passed out at the bottom of the back stairs, I sigh. Skipping class to deal with him is becoming a normal occurrence, even if I don't want it to be. I still don't know what I'm going to tell Uncle James if he finds out I'm not in class again.

"What the hell are you doing to me?" I mutter as I struggle to get him on his feet, seeing a thin trail of blood dripping from a cut on his forehead. "Shit."

My heart is pounding as I prop him against the wall and search his pockets. I pull out the key fob with shaky hands. I've been reading up on how to move an unconscious person, and from what I've read, it's safer to drag them rather than try to lift them up. I still stumble a couple of times. It's pretty inconvenient that these episodes seem to happen when there is no one around to help.

The drive to the hospital is short for once, but it's only because I'm driving faster than I should. The second I park the car in the emergency parking lot, Perkins starts groaning. His eyes open for a moment.

"Don't call Mom," he says, his voice firm before his eyes roll back in his head.

He has told me not to call his mother more than once. I don't know what he's hiding from her, but even if I wanted to call her, I couldn't. He's never given me her number, but he seems to forget that.

"Idiot," I mutter as I stagger under his weight again.

As soon as I am through the sliding doors of the emergency room, two nurses help get him onto one of the beds waiting in the hallway. The moment he's in their care, my adrenaline wears off and I start to panic. He shouldn't be passing out like he is.

"What's his name?" a nurse asks as she appears at my side while the other two wheel him down the hall.

"Weston Perkins. Can I go with him?" My heart hammers in my chest as I wipe my sweaty palms on my jeans.

"I'm sorry, honey," the nurse says, her hand landing on my shoulder. "Unless you're family, I can't let you go with him."

"I'm his boyfriend," I say, using the first thing that comes to mind. "He doesn't have any family around here. Neither do I. We're the only family each other has."

She gives me a pitying look before looking over her shoulder and nodding. "I'll take you to his room, but if they ask how you got there, you found it on your own, okay?"

I nod and smile. "Thank you."

She leads me through the swinging doors and down a few hallways. The whole time we're walking in silence, my mind is racing. I didn't think telling her he was my boyfriend would work. And then there's the panic that starts to rise when I think of him actually being my boyfriend.

There are a thousand reasons why West and I would never work. He drives me insane. He's not honest with me about what is going on with him...I never know when I'm going to have to drop everything to take care of him. The thought of dating him...loving him...is terrifying.

And yet, there's something enticing about it. Maybe it's the personality that he hides from everyone else. Those rare moments when he doesn't seem like the weight of the world is sitting on his shoulders. I like those moments the best. He lets his guard down and just lives.

The nurse opens the door to one of the rooms and motions for me to go inside. He's still unconscious, but a doctor is stitching up the cut on his head. I enter the room with a nod to the doctor before dropping down into the leather recliner.

It's going to be a while before he wakes up, if the bruising starting to appear on his forehead is anything to go by. I might as well make myself comfortable while I wait.

***

When he opens his eyes, I'm still sitting in the chair and scrolling through my phone. He takes a sharp inhale and hisses in pain as he struggles to sit up before falling back onto the pillows.

"Well, looks like Sleeping Beauty is finally awake," I say, getting up and walking to the edge of the bed.

The tension in my chest eases for the first time in hours as I look down at him. He's fine. At least, as fine as I suspect he can be with whatever he isn't telling me. Though none of the nurses who checked in on us had seemed concerned about him, I still am.

Now, the worry is dissipating as his confusion turns into a sour scowl. I sigh, already knowing where this is going. The surprised look in his eyes lingers, but I doubt it's a good surprise.

One step forward and three steps back, I think as I grab the glass of water from the side of the bed and hand it to him. I wrap my arm around his back, ignoring the tingles that race up and down my arm where our bodies touch. It feels like wildfire is consuming me whole, but I can't let him know that.

Instead, I keep him propped up while he drinks some of the water, wondering if my arm around him makes him feel the same way I do.

As soon as he can sit up on his own, I back up and watch him sip more of the water. He holds the glass in both his hands as if it is some sort of tether, but he stares at it like the water personally offends him.

"What are you doing here? Why am I in the hospital? Did you call my mother?"

"No, I didn't call your mother." I put more distance between us. "I found you passed out again and bleeding. Missed another class, so I'm expecting to have my ass chewed out, in case you care."

"I don't," he says, his tone sharp. "I didn't ask you to bring me here. You should have just taken me back up to my room or left me there. I would have been fine."

"Do you even hear yourself right now?" I ask, trying to shove the hurt I feel to the side. I wasn't expecting a warm welcome, but I also didn't think he was sure I was the kind of person who would leave him while he suffered.

If that's what he thinks of me, I can only imagine what else is going on in his head where I'm concerned.

"I didn't ask you to step in with your hero bullshit again," he says, crossing his arms at his chest. "I don't need you to keep doing this shit and I don't want you to."

"Fine. Next time I'll just call the fucking ambulance and leave you bleeding if that's what kind of person you think I am."

"I think you're too damn nosey for your own good, and the reason you keep hanging around is because helping the sick guy makes you feel good about yourself."

That one cuts deep. I nearly stumble backward as I stare at him, wondering who the hell is sitting in front of me. Perkins is not particularly a nice person, but I didn't think he was cruel, either. Now, I'm not so sure.

My heart aches for him in one way, though. He's burdened by the anger, the fear, the pain he carries on his chest, and it can't be easy. I want to go to him and hug him, insisting that whatever he's going through will get better soon. My head knows better though.

"Wow," I say, running a hand through my hair. "You really are a piece of work, aren't you? You think I'm still waiting in this fucking hospital for you so I can feel good about myself? Really?"

"Yes! You thrive on it. You walk around campus with this god complex. You puff out your chest, being all infallible and shit, like some fucking cape-wearing superhero."

"You know what?" I say, trying to keep the swell of emotions stuffed down. "You have no idea about what I'm going through because you don't ask. I have enough on my plate. I don't need to stand here and keep taking this shit from you just because you're miserable."

I toss his car fob onto the small table beside his bed before turning for the door.

Even though the ache in my chest has intensified, I don't take a second look at him. Being around him and feeling this way isn't worth it. Not even a little. I have more respect for myself than that.

Chapter 12

West

I'm still staring at the door long after Shane walked out. I don't know what I was thinking or why I treated him that way. He's only ever tried to help me and I keep throwing it back in his face.

With a wordless yell, I throw the glass in my hand across the room, only growing angrier as it shatters against the wall. Water drips down the wall as my head spins and my pulse races.

I'm an idiot. A world-class idiot who keeps shoving away the one person that wants to help me. The one person who keeps my secrets.

I don't know how I'm going to make this up to him. Then again, I don't know why I feel the need to make it up to him. He isn't my girlfriend or my family. He's only some guy from school that keeps shoving his nose where it doesn't belong.

Shane is irritating at best. He is too close, but he doesn't know what's happening either. Keeping my diagnosis a secret is getting harder with him sniffing around the way he is.

Then there is the part of me that wants to let him in further. I want his support as I go through this. That's the part of my mind that confuses me the most. It makes me want things I've never wanted before. And it pisses me off.

"What was that?" a nurse asks as she walks into the room, her eyes scanning around for any sign of damage. When she sees the broken glass, she gives me an understanding smile and opens up a cupboard to pull out a little broom and dustpan.

"I can clean that," I say, swinging my legs to the side to get out of bed.

As I do, the room starts to spin and I go tumbling back into the pillows on the bed. Bright lights shine above me and dots dance across my vision.

"Are you okay, honey?" she asks as she appears at my side. "You don't look like you're doing well. I just saw your boyfriend leave. Do you want me to call him back?"

I look at the car fob he'd tossed onto the little table, wondering how he was getting home. Then what the nurse said hits me. Shane told these people he's my boyfriend. He made them think that we were in a relationship so he could stay with me.

I don't know how that piece of information makes me feel. On one hand, I'm angry. I'm not in a relationship with him. Yes, I'm insanely attracted to him and there's no point in denying that anymore, but we're not together. I don't think we ever will be either. I'm not gay. There's nothing that exists like that between us.

"He has some things he needs to do," I say, not wanting to get into the intricacies of my relationship with Shane with her. "I'm fine though. I'll be fine."

"He looked pretty scared when he brought you in here. I suspected he's not your boyfriend, but he sure looks like he wants to be," she says, going back to the other side of the room and sweeping up the glass. "He's a good-looking boy, too. If he isn't your boyfriend, you should probably consider doing something about that."

My cheeks flame as I look out the window at the rain pouring down. The guilt crashes in waves over me, twice as strong as before. Shane gave me back the keys, which means he's bussing back to campus in the rain. He'll be soaked by the time he gets back to the dorm.

If I was nicer to him, he wouldn't have left.

"He's just a friend," I mutter, more to myself than to her.

Although, after what just happened between us a few minutes ago, I'm not sure I can even call him that.

I'm not sure I could have ever called him that. Over the several weeks I've known him, I've been a pretty terrible friend.

Looking back on all of it now, I wouldn't want to be friends with me either.

"Well, the doctor should be in to check those stitches soon now that you're awake and then once you sign some forms, you'll be free to go."

As she leaves the room, I'm already trying to figure out how I'm going to explain things to Shane.

***

The dorm is quiet when I walk back inside and there are only a few guys lounging about in the common room. I walk by them, my head dipped as I try to keep the bruises from being seen.

When I reach my floor, I look at Shane's door. It's shut, but there is light shining under the door. Even if he doesn't want to talk, he is still awake — or at least his roommate is — and I have some things to say to him.

For a moment, I consider letting it go and letting him move on with his life. I did a good job of creating a rift between us. All I need is for it to widen and then we can be free of each other. I can go back to only hiding my disease from Coach and the rest of the team.

Simple.

Except it's not because I still feel horrible for how I've treated him. I still feel like shit for pushing away the one person, outside of my family, who's cared about me.

"Fuck," I mutter, running a hand through my hair as I stand halfway between my door and his.

What I should do is go into my room and try to get some of my schoolwork done in the next few hours before going to bed and getting up early for practice. I should care more about getting my degree than what one guy down the hall thinks.

And then there's what I actually do.

With a sigh, I walk to his door and knock lightly. I can hear shuffling on the other side. The lock turns and the door opens. Shane appears in the thin crack between the door and the wall, his hair soaked and deep bags beneath his eyes.

"What do you want, Perkins?" he asks, pushing the wet hair out of his eyes.

I hate the way my heart beats harder in my chest, trying to break free from my ribcage.

"Can you come to my room? We need to talk."

Without giving him a chance to respond, I turn and take off down the hall. I hear the door shut and I hope he's following me but I'm too scared to look back.

When I open the door to my dorm, he is close behind me. As soon as the door shuts behind us, he crosses the room and leans against my desk, his arms crossing over his chest.

"How long did it take you to bus back here?" I ask, the guilt punching me in the gut.

"Only a few hours," he says, his tone biting as he smirks. "But you don't care about that, do you? You only care about feeling good after acting like the biggest jackass I've ever met. It's the same thing every time and I'm tired of it. I'm not going to absolve you of your guilt."

"I don't know what you want me to say."

Shane shakes his head. "That's just it, isn't it? You're so afraid of what other people think and hiding whatever the hell it is you're hiding that you're miserable. And that fucking misery means you drag other people down, trying to make them feel the same way you do! Do you even know how fucked up that is?"

The guilt tears me in half as I stand there staring at him. Angry Shane is almost as attractive as sweet Shane. I hate the warring feelings coursing through my body. I'm caught between begging him to forgive me and telling him to go to hell.

"I know it's fucked up," I say, taking a step closer to him. "You think I want to be this way? I hate what's happening to me and I hate that I can't talk about it, but you don't know what's on the line for me if I do."

"And you don't know what's on the fucking line for me if I keep dropping everything to help you. And I don't mind. I don't. Until you start treating me like shit!"

"You're right," I say, taking another step toward him. I'm not sure what I'm going to do when I get to him, but I don't miss the way his blue-green gaze slowly drags up and down my body. And I know he doesn't miss the way my gaze drops to his beautifully sinful mouth.

What would it be like to kiss another man? I wonder, while still trying to remind myself that we're mad at each other.

"You're right. I have no clue what's going on in your life and you don't know what's going on in mine. I haven't asked you to save my ass and you keep doing it. I don't know why. I've been nothing but an asshole."

"You don't know why I'm trying to be there for you, so your response is to treat me like shit? Are you for real right now? Everyone has shit going on in their lives. It doesn't mean we get a free pass to treat people like they're less than." Shane pushes off the desk, standing tall. "I didn't RSVP to your pity party, so I'm getting the fuck out of here."

Before he can say anything else, I cross the room to him. His eyes widen as I crowd his space until he's leaning against the desk again. My breathing is shallow as I look down at him, wondering if I'm really about to do this.

Fuck it. I grab him by the hips, pulling his body against mine and crashing my mouth into his.

Shane's mouth feels soft and warm against mine as his hands travel up my back before his fingers weave through my hair. He tastes so good, like cinnamon sugar, as our tongues collide. Our mouths move together, my hands gripping his hips as he pulls my hair lightly. He moans into my mouth and I close my eyes, losing myself in him. It's only when I feel my achingly hard cock rub against his that my eyes fly open and I jump back like I've been lit on fire.

Shane looks at me with surprise for a moment, his lips red and wet with saliva, before he exhales, his body deflating in defeat. He gives me a single nod and walks out of my dorm.

When the door clicks into place behind him, I sink to the ground and stare at the ceiling.

I don't know how I'm going to fix this one.

Chapter 13

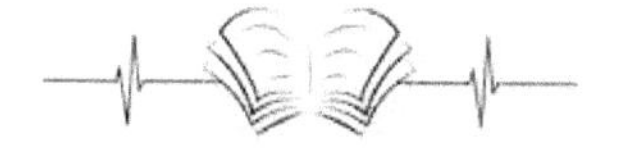

Shane

I try to convince myself that it will be easy for me to avoid West like the plague. Bright and early Saturday morning, I don my running shoes and hit the trail. There's a strange comfort in maneuvering around rocks, mud, dirt, and other obstacles in the way. I'm not the only runner doing this today, but I still feel alone, one with nature. The uneven terrain makes me run slower and exert greater mental and physical effort, but I love the challenge of the trail.

It's amazing how the dawn chorus starts with chirping, whistling, and trilling, and is then joined by twittering and tweeting, creating a beautiful symphony in nature — the robins, thrushes, and other birds, the orchestra.

I stand in awe as the sun rises in all its glory, with a burst of vibrant blue and violets, yellow, orange, and red in the cloudless sky. It often confounds me that in the midst of all this beauty, there exists turmoil in the world, turmoil in my heart.

My mind inevitably swings to thoughts of West. So much for giving my head a reprieve from thoughts of him. I feel more than a mere attraction to him at this point and I don't even know why. He hasn't endeared himself to me — he's not even nice — so why am I affected by him this much? He has me wrapped around his little finger, and he doesn't even know it. Unbelievable! Is it some internal flaw I have and am only now realizing it? How could my body — my heart — have such a visceral response to him? To say I'm baffled by my feelings for the guy is an understatement.

Ethan checks in on me that afternoon, but I think he's dealing with some boy drama of his own. He hasn't given me the details, but I suspect he and Maddox have some history and things are coming to a head.

On Sunday, I finish up the assignments that are due this week and spend the rest of the day reading *Little Women*, one of my mom's favorite books. I've read it before, but I feel compelled to give it a re-read. Then I come across, "Be worthy love, and love will come," and it punches me in the solar plexus. When was the last time I felt worthy of love? That's an easy one to answer; it was when my mom took her last breath in my arms. She raised me in the best way she knew how, and there wasn't a day in my life when she didn't make me her personal concern. Not a single day went by that she didn't tell me she loved me. What a woman Linda Johnson was, leaving behind a mom-sized hole in my heart. With no siblings, a father whom I never knew, and grandparents who are keeping my mother company in what I'd like to think is paradise, there's no one in this world who loves me. At least, not in the way that I need. Uncle James might be blood, but he isn't truly my family. His concern for me is more out of duty and obligation, rather than of an emotion coming straight from his heart.

I'd stupidly thought West could have developed genuine feelings for me, like I have for him. But the only person I'd fooled was myself. One of the biggest mistakes a gay man could make is falling for a straight guy. I'd been taught that lesson before, but apparently, I'd never learned it.

West kissed me.

He fucking kissed *me*.

How can I reconcile the fact that he's straight with him kissing me? *Me*?

The kiss was amazing, so much better than my fantasies. I can still taste West's mint-flavored tongue, feel his stubble rubbing against my cheek, and smell the woody undertones of his cologne. And the crazy part is he seemed to enjoy it just as much. He was hard for me.

I haven't known what to think since that kiss, and I can't even talk to anyone about it. West presents himself as straight, but I'm not going to lie, a part of me is hopeful he's at least bisexual and just hasn't figured it out yet. At least I'd have a fighting chance to be with him if he's bi.

But, if he's straight, and the kiss was merely an aberration, I'm fucked.

Too soon, Monday comes around and there's no more hiding in my room or running from my problems on the trails.

Uncle James is waiting for me by his car, a bouquet of flowers in his hand. He rests his hand on my shoulder and squeezes hard. I look up at him, trying to blink away the tears that brim my eyes.

Three years after my grandfather died and this day still hasn't gotten any easier.

"I miss him too," my uncle says as we get in the car, ready for the drive to the cemetery.

The tombstones never make me feel anything other than uncomfortable. Uncle James puts the flowers down and takes his hat off, holding it against his chest.

"It's been years, Dad, and I still miss you like crazy," he says, his voice sounds choked as he wipes his eyes. "I don't know how we're supposed to keep doing this without you."

"I don't know either."

It's during times like these my uncle seems the most human, the most approachable, to me.

My grandmother died nearly twelve years ago. After her passing, my grandpa had come to live with me and my mom. He had been the father figure in my life for a long time and when he died, nobody was sure I was ever going to be okay again.

"I miss him," I say as we walk back to the car an hour later. "I wish he was still here. I miss Mom too."

Uncle James puts his hat back on and starts the car. "I do too. I don't know what to do with you, Shane. I keep hearing you've been missing classes. You can't keep doing that. I know I've been hard on you, but you need to show the disciplinary committee you're changing."

"Wow." I lean my head against the cold window. "I thought we might have been able to have one afternoon together where you didn't make me feel like a complete failure, but I guess I was wrong about that."

"Shane, don't be melodramatic. You need to get your head into it. Work harder and show up to class. The end of the semester is coming up soon and if you aren't doing what they want you to do, they will kick you out. There's nothing I'm going to be able to do at that point."

"You think I don't know that?" I turn to face him. "I'm acutely aware of the fact that my entire future rests on being here and getting the disciplinary committee on my side."

"Then stop messing around."

"I've had some shit going on." My tone is sharp as I glare at the side of his head. Right this minute, I'm more grateful than ever that my uncle and mom didn't get along. He was her big brother and when she'd gotten pregnant with me during her first year of college, he never let her live it down. They were always at odds with each other, as he constantly nitpicked the choices she made, especially on the way she was raising me. Can you imagine what my life would have been like if I'd been around him when I was growing up? Hopefully, my time at TU will fly by quickly and I'll graduate with honors and be out from under his constant scrutiny.

"I don't care what you've had going on. Get it together."

We fall silent as he drives back to the campus. I have nothing left to say to him on the matter.

All I can hope is that the rest of the semester finishes without any more problems.

***

When I get back to the dorm, West is waiting downstairs. He looks up as I walk in, tucking his phone into his pocket and giving me a sharp nod. I sigh, torn between going to my room, steering clear of him, and kissing him again.

"What?" I ask as I stop in front of him, my own hands in my pockets because I don't trust myself not to grab him and drag him to me for another kiss.

"We need to talk about whatever the hell happened on Friday." His voice is low as other students descend the stairs and enter the common room. "I've been freaking out all weekend and you've been avoiding me."

I raise my eyebrow and look at him. "Can you blame me? There's a whole steaming pile of shit between us and then the basic differences of who we are as people on top of that. Isn't that right, Perk the Jerk?"

He winces. "Please, just come up to my room and we can talk about this."

"And what if I don't want to talk?" I don't want to be strung along by a man who isn't comfortable with whatever is happening with his sexuality.

"Then we don't have to, but I don't think we'll ever talk again if that happens."

I don't want that to happen, so I follow him up the stairs to our floor, trying not to stare at his ass when other people pass us. We don't say anything until we are in his dorm and the door is shut firmly behind us.

"I kissed you." West looks at me, confusion clearly written all over his face. "I'm straight and I kissed you and I want to kiss you again. And I'm freaking the fuck out."

"Well, there are a couple different answers." I sit on the edge of his bed and stretch my legs out in front of me. "You're either straight and curious, completely overwhelmed by whatever drugs they gave you, or bisexual."

Perkins only looks more distressed as he paces back and forth in front of me. "How am I supposed to know the answer to that?"

"That's on you to figure out. I can't tell you what you are or aren't."

"And what if I am bisexual?"

"Congratulations and welcome to the alphabet mafia, I guess." I smirk as I fall back on his bed and cross my arms behind my head. "Look, I know it's confusing as fuck and only made worse by the fact that you're a football player where anybody who is not straight and cisgender is a problem. But it's on you to figure it out. I can't figure it out for you."

As much as I don't want to be his experiment, I still do. If it means being close to him and being the person who's there for him, I'm more than happy to be his dirty little secret.

I sit up, not wanting to be too relaxed in his bed. That would only invite all kinds of thoughts into my head, thoughts I don't need right now. Like the way his erection had pressed against me. I definitely don't need to be thinking about that.

"I don't know how to deal with this on top of everything else." West sinks to the ground and leans back against the wall. He stretches his legs out in front of him and runs his hand through his dark hair.

I look at the stubble on his cheeks, wondering when the last time he shaved was. I want to feel that rough skin against my own as our mouths merge and his large hands sit possessively on my hips again.

But kissing him right now would be the worst thing I could do.

"West," I say softly, taking in the distress on his face. "You need to calm the fuck down. This isn't the end of the world."

"What happens to us now that we've kissed? Do we just pretend it never happened and go on with our lives?"

"I'm attracted to you, West. I'm not going to bother denying it since I kissed you back. But I know who I am and who I'm attracted to. Hell I know why it's you. But the thing is, you're still figuring all of it out, which means the ball is in your court. It's up to you what happens next."

"I don't know what I want."

"Nobody ever really does."

There's a long silence as we stare at each other. Neither one of us knows what to say to the other. I wish that I could tell him that it gets easier, but figuring out who you are never does. I was lucky enough to grow up with a mother who encouraged me to be who I was.

"Tell me," West says, and I immediately know what he wants. It has become our little thing where he asks me what I've been reading and wants to know which quote from the book resonates with me.

"It's from Oscar Wilde's *The Picture of Dorian*. 'You will always be fond of me. I represent to you all the sins you never had the courage to commit.'"

"Oh, fuck." West runs his hands through his hair again.

Yes, West, oh fuck. Because that quote describes both of us to a tee. I want you to sin with me, pretty please.

I don't dare speak my thoughts aloud. He's already ambivalent about his feelings for me, so I don't want to tip him over to the side of 'I can't be with Shane because I'm unequivocally a straight man'.

"Shane, I don't know what the fuck I'm doing. This is going to sound horrible, but I think I want to pretend that kiss never happened. I don't have it in me to deal with it on top of everything else."

"That's fine," I mutter. With my chest tight and aching, I stand and walk to the door. "You have as much time as you want to figure it out. If you change your mind, West, you know where to find me."

When the door closes behind me, I hear the crash of glass thrown against the door and the broken pieces falling to the floor. It mirrors the way my heart feels, like it's been slammed against wood, shattering as it hits the floor. For a moment, I consider going back to West and sitting with him for as long as it takes for him to be okay again.

Unfortunately, time is limited and as much as I want to be the person who's there for him, he's not ready for that yet.

CHAPTER 14

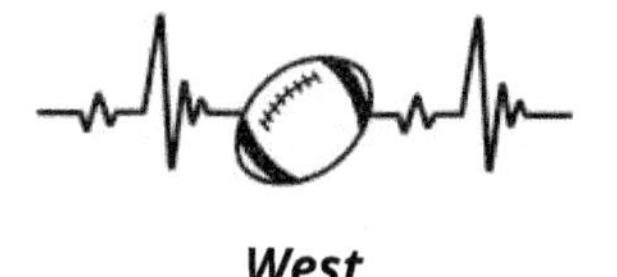

West

After weeks of medications making me sick, I don't know how much more I can take.

I stumble back to my bed from the bathroom and throw myself down onto the mattress. I sling my arm over my face. Even with the curtains drawn and the lights off, the room is still too bright. My head is pounding, and it feels like I'm sucking on cotton.

Attending classes today isn't going to happen. I doubt it's going to happen tomorrow, either. Hell, it hasn't happened for the last two days. I need to be better by Saturday night for the game. Coach will be pissed if I miss it and the last thing I want to do is disappoint him, especially if scouts are going to be there.

With a groan, I roll over onto my stomach, but quickly realize it's a bad idea. Within moments, I'm up and running to the bathroom again.

When I'm done throwing up all of my internal organs, I remove my shorts and lean against the cold wall of the shower, turning on the tap. Icy water cascades over me, but it does little to shock my system into functioning semi-normally again.

I'm still leaning on the wall when I hear pounding on my door. For a few seconds, I consider telling whoever it is to go away. Instead, I crawl out of the shower and use the edge of the sink to pull myself into an upright position and pull on a dry pair of shorts. I'm already trying to figure out how to explain my appearance as I walk to the door and pull it open.

"Figured you might want this." Shane brushes past me and crosses the room to drop a stack of papers on my desk. "You missed a lot of work. Some projects are due soon and one of the professors said you haven't been to any of his office hours to discuss your topic."

"You didn't have to do that." I sit on the edge of my bed. The room is still spinning.

Even though I'm happy Shane's here, especially after what happened between us only a few days ago, I don't want him to see me like this. I don't want him anywhere near me when I still haven't figured out how I feel about him. Hell, I haven't even figured out if I'm straight or bi, or maybe something in-between.

"Look, I have places I need to be, so if you're good with what I brought you, I'll be on my way." Shane looks at me with those intense eyes of his, as if he wants to say more. He sighs and walks to the door instead, metaphorically biting his tongue on whatever else it is he wants to tell me.

"Shane, don't go."

The tension in the room increases as I stare at his back, wondering if I'm enough to make him stay. I want him to step away from the door and say he'll stay with me, even though I have no clue what it means if he does.

"Please, Shane...don't go."

He turns and faces me but his eyes are still averted.

"Tell me," I breathe.

Shane regards me for several beats, his face void of emotion. "I've got two from *The Alchemist*, but I'll summarize them since I haven't gotten the chance to commit them to memory. The first is, *when you want something, the entire fucking universe conspires to make sure you get it*." He smiles for the first time since coming to my room. "The word fucking isn't in the original." Then, he continues, "And the second is, *because life is the moment we're living right now. If we give ourselves a fucking chance to concentrate on the present, then you'll be fucking happy*. Again, the word fucking isn't in the original."

"I want to be happy, Shane." What I don't say out loud is I think I want to be happy with him.

"West," he says with a sigh, and my heart races. He called me West for the first time a few days ago. The only other person who called me West was my grandmother.

She was the only one who ever really knew and accepted me for everything I am. Losing her had seemed impossible to recover from, but I've learned to live with the vacuum she left in my life, only to find out I was dying too.

Shane seems to go back and forth between what he wants to say. He drops his backpack to the floor before taking a seat at my desk.

"I don't know what to think about all of this." He runs his hand through his tresses and as his hair catches the light in my room, it's the first time I notice its subtle shade of orange. "You know that, don't you? I understand you're questioning your sexuality right now and that's fine, but fuck, West, being around you while you figure it out isn't easy for me."

My stomach starts churning and I don't know if it's because I'm about to throw up again or because Shane makes me feel something that the girls I've dated never have. The fact I've been hiding my diagnosis from him still continues to eat away at me. Over the last couple of nights, I've thought about telling him, but whenever I imagine saying the words, all I can see is him either pitying me or getting up and walking out the door.

"I know." I reach for my bottle of water and play with the cap. I need to keep my hands busy, keep myself distracted from the intoxicating scent of his body spray. "Shane..." I take a deep breath and blow it out. "I'm dying."

His eyes widen as he glances over at the line of pill bottles on one of my shelves. I can see him starting to put the pieces together, trying to figure out what exactly is wrong with me. The gears are turning in his head as he stands and starts pacing the floor. He puts his hands on his hips as he exhales and pauses in the middle of the room, turning to look at me.

"For real?" His usually deep, rich voice is small. It's the tone that breaks my heart. I wish I'd told him sooner. Maybe it would have changed things between us. Maybe we would have gotten along better and spent more time together.

I don't want to waste any more of the time we have left together, but I don't know if I can be anything more than friends with him.

"It's called juvenile hemochromatosis, a disorder that has seriously affected my liver. Found out I had the disease not too long ago. Diagnosed with liver failure the first time you came with me to the hospital. Need a new liver." Even the thought of speaking in complete sentences saps the strength from my body.

Shane looks as shell-shocked as I still feel. Being acutely aware of the fact that you're dying is nothing someone is okay with. I don't expect him to be okay right away, either.

I hate that there is nothing I can do to comfort him. Getting up and hugging him would only continue to blur the already blurred lines between us. I watch as he resumes pacing, taking in the new information.

"Why didn't you tell me sooner?"

I shrug. There are a thousand reasons why I've never told anyone anything about my diagnosis.

"I guess it all boils down to the fact that I want to actually live with whatever time I have left rather than sitting around and having people worry over and pity me."

"They worry about you because they give a shit, West," Shane says as he sits down at the desk and runs a hand over his face. He looks exhausted.

"One minute." I lurch to my feet and rush for the bathroom.

I try not to think about Shane sitting on the other side of the door, listening to me vomit. Once I'm done, I get up and brush my teeth before staggering back out into the bedroom.

Shane is still sitting in the same position, but there's a pale tinge to his skin. He looks like he's going to be the next one to get sick.

"I don't want people to treat me differently." I toss myself on my bed and sling my arm over my face, trying to block out the light again. "I don't want them to treat me like I'm made of glass. And then there's what will happen if Coach finds out. I'll lose every chance I have at a future in the NFL."

"You've got to get better, West." Shane's tone is almost beseeching, desperate. "Are you on the transplant list?"

"I got put on it but the doctor seems cautiously optimistic. There're a lot of factors that go into getting a new liver and while I am a good candidate, I'm not at the top of the list yet."

Shane scoffs, and I hear the chair squeak as he stands. I can hear him pacing back and forth again. He makes a couple of laps around the room with his pacing before the chair squeaks again. I peek at him from beneath my arm to see him sitting and taking deep breaths.

"Stop acting like it's the end of the world." I sit up and back myself against the wall since the bed doesn't have a headboard.

"Sorry, it's just a little hard to find out that the guy who I want to —" Shane cuts himself off before he could finish saying...what?

That I'm the guy he wants to date? Fuck? What is it? Surprisingly, the thought of us dating or fucking or both doesn't seem outrageous at all.

"I'm trying to keep the faith that I'll make it to the NFL," I say, glossing over the comment that Shane didn't finish, but which has caused him to feel embarrassed, judging by the flush that is creeping across his cheeks. I don't think he meant to say it and it's easier to not address it. "I'm on dialysis and all these meds that are making me blow chunks. Doctors are doing their best to keep me alive for as long as they possibly can."

"Yeah, and do any of your doctors really know how long that's going to be? Do they know you're pushing your body to its limits every week while you play football and then still expect your body to be able to keep you going?"

"Calm down."

"Then start acting like what you've been going through is a problem!" Shane shouts as he stands up.

"I know it's a fucking problem, but there's nothing I can do about it. Sooner or later, I'm going to be dead. People won't give a shit any more than they do now."

Shane's eyes are shining as he turns away from me. "Nice to know you think nobody gives a shit about you."

"This is exactly what I meant about treating me differently." My tone is sharp as I glare at his back. "You're going to fuck right off out of my life now, right? Same as everyone else would do if they knew the truth."

Shane turns to face me, his eyes red-rimmed. "You really don't know anything about me, so shut your fucking mouth. I sat by my mother every fucking day for the last year while the cancer consumed her. When chemotherapy and radiation stopped working and the rest of my family bailed because it was too hard to deal with, I was the one that was still there!"

"I'm sorry." I feel like the wind has been knocked out of my lungs. He couldn't have hit me harder if he had sucker punched me. "I didn't know."

"Of course you didn't know, West. You act like the only person you give a shit about is yourself."

He's right. I know he's right. I push people away. I always have to some extent, but it's gotten worse since my diagnosis. And for the last few weeks, the only person I've cared about is myself. Shane came to me looking for help to clear his name with the dean, but I sent him away because it would have exposed my secret.

"Look, you're an asshole, and being sick doesn't excuse that, but I'm not going to let you go through this alone either, not when nobody else even knows you're sick. Does your mother know?"

I swallow hard, the guilt washing over me in massive waves. "She knows I've got juvenile hemochromatosis but she doesn't know it has reached the organ failure stage."

"That's not the kind of thing you don't tell your mother."

I shrug and look out the window, watching as clouds overtake the sun and rain begins to fall. "It is if you knew my mother. Look, just promise me you're not going to tell anyone. I can't risk this messing up my future any more than it already has. Scouts are at the football games and they're watching me. I need to do well and I can't do that if I'm worried about you telling people what's wrong with me."

"I'm not going to tell anyone." He slumps in the chair as if all of the energy has been drained from his body. "Like I said, I'm not going to leave you alone to deal with this either."

"You don't have to," I say. "I'm fine on my own."

He scoffs and grabs the TV remote, turning it on and finding some terrible action movie. "From where I'm sitting, you're not doing fine."

As I watch him sitting there, processing everything I told him, I think he might be right.

CHAPTER 15

Shane

Before I'd met West, the last thing I would have wanted to do on a Saturday night is sit through a football game. But I've slowly but surely come to appreciate the sport. He's something else when he's on the field. It's like everything else just seems to fade away. Who could even tell he's not in perfect health? I don't think I would have ever guessed had I not already known.

I want to tell him just how great he is when the game ends. Forty-five minutes pass and he still isn't by his car, but I know something just must have come up. I wait patiently for him, leaning against the car and scrolling through my phone.

Since he'd told me about his diagnosis a couple days ago, I have scoured the internet, looking for any information I could find to tell me there was hope. All articles pointed in one direction at his stage. Either death or a liver transplant.

"You ready for the party?" West asks as he appears at my side and unlocks the car.

"Sure." I know going to a party is still a monumentally bad idea because shit can happen, which will not go down well with the disciplinary committee. But I just can't bring myself to turn down spending time with him. "Where is it?"

"Just outside of town. It's a tailgate in some guy's field to celebrate our win."

"Sounds like a great idea," I say dryly.

Laughing, West starts the car, his arm draping over the back of my seat as he reverses the vehicle out of his parking space and into the line of traffic leaving the stadium. I try not to let the brush of his fingers on my shoulder bother me as I settle into my seat. His arm is gone within a few moments and I release the breath I've been holding.

The drive is filled with rock music and tension. I want to ask him more questions about his diagnosis and what it all means, but I doubt my questions would be kindly received.

West pulls off the dark highway about half an hour into our drive. The road turns to dirt and weeds as he navigates through the field. The music grows louder as we approach a wide circle of vehicles parked around a group of people. West switches off the engine but leaves his headlights on.

"You're fine with being here, right?"

"I'd rather shove splinters beneath my nails," I quip as I get out of the car and follow him to a cooler of drinks. West opens the lid and gestures at the drinks nestled in ice.

"Water."

He grabs two bottles of water before returning to his car. He leans against the hood, watching the people around us dance and drink. As I join him, he tosses me one of the bottles before cracking his open and taking a long sip.

I can't help but drink him in. His hair is still damp from the shower he took after the game. I want to run my fingers through it. I want to touch him as assurance that he's here and everything is going to be okay — that he isn't going to die. But I can't. My dick twitches in my jeans as West's shirt rises, showing off the muscled planes of his stomach. Our kiss comes scorching through my memory.

I subtly adjust myself and consider dumping the icy water over my own head.

"Liquid Flames is going to be performing an acoustic set," West says, nodding to a guy on a tailgate tuning a guitar.

"They're doing pretty good for themselves." I stand beside him for what seems like an eternity, taking sips of water and listening to the songs blasting from somebody's speakers. The headlights drown the stars out.

People are already drunk, stumbling to and from their cars while their designated drivers watch them.

"Want to go for a walk?" West asks after dodging another drunk person determined to spill their drink on someone.

"Sure." I secretly wish he'd asked if I wanted to go home.

He leads the way away from the party and deeper into the field. There's a path worn into the ground that he shines the flashlight from his phone on. Behind us, I can hear the sounds of the bonfire crackling in the night as the stereo music cuts out and Liquid Flames gets ready to play.

When we reach the fence, West hauls himself up to sit on top of it. I stand beside him, leaning back against the fence and looking up at the stars.

"How did you know you were interested in men?" His voice is barely more than a whisper.

I smile. "I've always been interested in men on some level or another. There was always something about a man that was more appealing than a woman. It just took some time to figure myself out."

"So you didn't just wake up one day and know you were gay?"

I try to think of the right thing to say, but I know there's nothing that will make this journey easier for him. His sexuality is something I'm not going to be able to figure out for him, even if I want to.

"Nope. I didn't just wake up and know I was gay. It was always there. It just took some time to see it for what it was."

"How did your family react?"

I look back at him. "Mom didn't care. She said that as long as I'm happy and in a healthy relationship, she doesn't care who I'm with."

"What did your dad say?"

"Don't know, don't care," I say with a shrug. "He ditched the family shortly after I was born. My grandparents were cool with it. My grandfather said he should've been gay so he wouldn't have to deal with my grandmother's bitching. Grandma smacked him with her cane."

West laughs. "I wish it would be that easy with my parents. Not that I'm saying I'm gay because I'm not. Maybe bi." He expelled a breath with a gush. "I don't even fucking know."

"You don't have to know right now." I look away from him, hating the way my heart races in my chest each time he laughs. "You don't think your family would accept you?"

"My mom and dad have never understood me. They're both academics with dreams of me entering academia as well. Neither of them understands football or why I like it. I don't think they've come to one game this year, even though my mom and I have breakfast together every week. It's more of a chance for her to criticize all my life choices."

"You don't think they'd accept you bringing a man home?" Even Uncle James had accepted my sexuality without question, even though he's a beast about most things.

"I don't think they would support me doing anything other than what they want me to do."

He looks like a lost boy in that moment, like he has no clue where he's supposed to be in life, where he fits in. I want to reach out and hug him, but instead, I stuff my hands in my pockets and keep my mouth shut. Being here with him is a risky game I'm all too eager to lose.

"I don't even know how to start having that conversation with them...if I ever figure it out for myself. And then there's whatever the team will say. I want to think most of the guys would be okay with it but gay men and football don't exactly go together."

I nod. "You're right. They don't. I wish I could tell you everyone is going to be cool with it and accept you as you are, but that wouldn't be the truth. People are horrible and you're going to get called all kinds of slurs at some point in your life."

"How do you do it?"

"I decided I would rather let all the bullshit roll off of me than spend my life miserable in a closet, pretending to be someone I'm not. It's the price I pay to live my truth and it's worth it."

His lips press together in a thin line as he nods. "Tell me, Shane."

I study him for a moment before I respond. I'm going out on a limb, inviting him to see what has been playing on a loop in my head for the last several days.

"I'll tell you one of my personal mantras this time around, not one from the book I'm currently reading. It goes, 'It doesn't matter who you want to fuck, so long as you know you're loved.'"

We fall silent for a few minutes as he considers what I said. West stares down at the water bottle in his hands, twisting the plastic.

"I'm terrified I'm not going to have a clue who I am before I die," West says softly before he slides down from the fence.

I turn to face him. "I know I said I was around if you change your mind about pretending that kiss never happened, West. I already know your deepest, darkest secrets. If you want somebody to fool around with while you figure out your sexuality, I'm here and you know I'm not going to out you."

He looks like a deer in the headlights as he glances at me before walking away. "You always have to make things more complicated, don't you?"

"I don't know how that is making it more complicated," I say as I follow him back toward his car. "Seemed like it was going to make it easier."

West shakes his head as we near the ring of vehicles and the people dancing. "It's a bad idea, Shane. I appreciate the offer, but it's not going to happen."

I nod, not having anything else to say. I hate the way my chest tightens as I follow him. The offer was the riskiest game I had played yet. If he and I started hooking up, my feelings for him would only grow, and then one of two things could happen. He could realize he doesn't want me, or he could die.

"Are you ready to head back to the dorms?" West asks.

"Yeah. I have some work I need to get done, and coming here was a bad idea to begin with."

Between the football game and taking care of West, I'm trying to make sure I don't put my grades at risk. If I don't spend the next day trying to get caught up, I'm going to start failing.

West doesn't say much to me on the drive back to campus. We walk together up the stairs to our floor before parting ways.

When I open the door to my dorm, Ethan is wide awake and pacing the floor. He looks manic as he runs his hands through his hair.

"Ethan? You okay, man?"

"Sure," Ethan says, sounding strained as he stops pacing and flops down onto his bed. "I might murder Maddox soon, but that's nothing new."

"What's wrong?" I kick off my jeans and collapse onto my own bed.

"I'm tutoring him and I've never met a more infuriating person in my life. Some things are barely worth it for the money. If it didn't pay so well, I'd steal a car just for the sake of running him over."

He starts laughing and groans into his pillow. I laugh with him and start talking about the party and all the other people there that he could run over as well. For the first time since starting at TU, I feel as if I've found a friendship that will last a lifetime.

I realize my relationship with West could easily be more than friendship, it could be everything, even though I know I'm only inviting heartbreak into my life.

CHAPTER 16

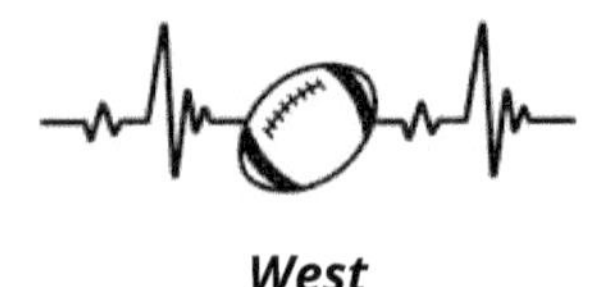

West

I've spent most of the night awake and thinking about Shane's offer in between rounds of throwing up. If I'm going to figure out my sexuality with anyone, he would be my first choice, but I don't want to jeopardize the only honest relationship I have in my life.

I take my meds, brush my teeth, and head out the door to meet my mom for our Sunday breakfast.

Mom is sitting at the table when I arrive, food is already in front of her. I eye the steak and eggs she ordered for me, wondering if I would be able to keep it down.

"How are you doing?" she asks as I sit across from her and start sipping at my water.

"Fine. School is going well, and football is pretty good too. There was a scout at my game last night, but I didn't see you or Dad there."

She gives me a small smile as she picks at her avocado toast. "We weren't able to make it to the game. Maybe we'll be at your next one."

It's always the same with her and Dad. They'll always be at the next game, but they never actually show up. I stopped hoping for them to watch me play a long time ago. I still don't see the point of waiting for something I know is never going to happen. They don't care about football and I can't make them proud of me for it.

"That's great, Mom." I might as well just accept the fact that things won't change. Arguing with my mother never ends well. It usually results in my being iced out and only communicating with Dad while she sits on the other end of the phone and complains about everything I did wrong that led to that moment.

"Are you sure you're alright? You look like you're skin and bones. And you're jaundiced."

I sigh and push my eggs around, trying to delay answering her. "I'm fine, Mom. Just not feeling that well. There's a lot of stress with school right now. I'll call my doctor soon and figure out if it's anything I have to worry about or not."

Mom's lips purse together as she grabbed her handbag from the chair beside her. I watch as she digs around inside, producing her wallet and opening it to toss a couple bills on the table.

"What are you doing?" I eye her as she stands up and slings her bag over her arm.

She doesn't say anything to me, her lips still pursed as she pulls out her phone and dials a number.

"Hi, Dr. Sullivan. I'm calling on behalf of Weston Perkins. I'm his mother and I have a concern. He's lost a considerable amount of weight in the last month and his skin has a yellow tinge to it."

Time seems to stop around me as I watch her eyes widen as she looks at me. I know Dr. Sullivan can't disclose my medical history without my permission, but it doesn't mean she isn't telling my mother there's something wrong with me.

"Okay, thank you. I'll meet you there."

She ends the call and tosses her phone back into her purse. I don't like the look on her face as she looks down at me.

"You would think after all these years, you would tell your own mother when there's something seriously wrong with you. I knew I shouldn't have believed you the last time you said you were fine. Now go get your ass in the car. We're going to the hospital."

I'm jolted by the force of her words. My mother and I haven't had a close relationship in years, but she'd never, not even for a sliver of a moment, spoken to me in that way before.

"Mom, I'm fine. I don't need to go to the hospital." My voice sounds weak and feeble even to my own ears. Over the last few weeks, I've noticed the weight I'm losing, but the yellow tint to my skin had to have appeared overnight. I hadn't even noticed it myself. If I'd known, I would have made an excuse to skip breakfast. Nothing escapes my mother's scrutiny. Nothing.

"Weston, get in the car."

With a sigh, I get up and follow her to the parking lot. She doesn't say another word to me as she drives to the hospital. She sniffles and I can see the tears running down her cheeks. I feel like I'm the worst son in the world as she walks with me into the hospital and goes to speak with one of the nurses.

Before I know it, I'm in a private room with a hospital gown being shoved into my hands. I look at the thin piece of fabric as Mom sits down on a chair in the corner and calls my dad. Despite my parents having successful careers their entire lives, Dad's family is from old money. In times like these, I'm grateful for it. It means I don't have to suffer the stares of other patients in the waiting room.

"We'll need you to get changed so we can start running some tests," a nurse says as she walks into the room with a bright smile. "After that, the doctor will take a look and tell you what's going on."

"It's liver failure," I say as I head toward the bathroom. "Early-stage liver failure. I already know what's wrong with me."

Mom starts sobbing. I feel another twist of guilt.

"We still need you to get changed so we can see if there's any worsening in your condition," the nurse says.

If it's my time to die, I don't want to bother with all the tests they're going to run. Staying in the hospital and being in pain for days on end isn't any sort of way to live.

But instead of putting up a fight, I get changed into the hospital gown and head back out to be poked and prodded like a prize pig.

***

"No. There's no way. I didn't even know he was sick. How can this be happening?" Mom wails as she collapses into a chair. Dad sits down on the arm of the chair, holding her tight.

"I'm sorry," Dr. Sullivan says as she stands by my bedside. "Stage-four liver failure is serious. I'm going to start making some calls to see if I can get you moved up the transplant list."

"Don't think it's going to do much good if you haven't been able to get me one yet." I lean back on my pillows.

I'm trying not to think about the diagnosis and how much worse everything has gotten in just a few weeks. It doesn't seem long enough for the liver failure to progress this rapidly, and yet it has.

"There is more priority placed on a young man in his early twenties who has just reached stage-four liver failure," Dr. Sullivan says as she looks at my parents. "I'm sorry to have to deliver the news to you this way, but we caught it early enough for them to bump you up the list."

"What if I don't want to be bumped up the list?" I ask before I have time to consider the words that are coming out of my mouth.

"Don't say that!" Mom leaps to her feet and storms across the room to stand beside my bed. "You can't say things like that, Weston. You want to live. You still have college to finish and I'm sure there's some nice girl you're going to meet soon. What about getting married, starting your career, starting a family?"

"Mom, I didn't mean it like that." I scrub a hand down my face, wishing I'd had more time alone to process the new diagnosis. "Why don't you and Dad go get some dinner while I talk to my coach about missing practice this week?"

I'm barely keeping it together as I say the words, but I need her to leave the room. Anger is boiling to the surface and if I don't get some space, I'm going to snap.

"Test me," Mom says, looking at Dr. Sullivan. "See if I'm a match."

"Me too," Dad says.

Dr. Sullivan nods. "I'll be able to test both of you in the morning, but until then, I will suggest everyone gets some rest while I make some calls."

"Mom, you and Dad should go get some dinner." I'm desperate for some time alone.

Dad takes one look at me and nods. I breathe a sigh of relief. At least somebody understands. He gets up from the chair and goes over to my mom, leading her out of the room as she cries into his shoulder.

"I'm going to make those calls, but you hit the button there if you need any help," Dr. Sullivan says as she grabs her clipboard and heads out of the room.

The moment she's gone, I walk over to the door and slam it shut. I try to take deep breaths, but it doesn't work. The world is closing in around me and there's nothing I can do. I'm going to die. I'm not even twenty-one yet and I'm going to die. There's nothing that they're going to be able to do to save me.

Then there's Coach. There's no way to keep the news from him any longer. He's going to bench me until doctors clear me and even then, I'll be lucky if he ever lets me play again after lying to him.

There's nothing I can do to stop any of it from happening. I feel betrayed by my own body and by what it's doing to me. I wish there was another way out of this. I catch sight of myself in the mirror across the room. The muscle I packed on over the summer is now gone. I can see the yellow tint to my skin. Maybe I was just blind to what has been happening to me, in denial, but now I've got no choice but to face it.

The person staring back at me is dying and their life depends on a list of transplant donors.

It doesn't seem like the man in the mirror can be me, but he is.

"Fuck!" I scream as I grab the lamp and hurl it at the mirror.

The mirror and the lamp shatter, erasing the image of the dying man. Shards of glass rain down onto the floor as I slump against the wall. My chest is tight, and my heart is racing. It feels like I can't get enough oxygen into my lungs.

"I'm going to die," I whisper as I stare at the pile of glass.

I take a few deep breaths — as deep as I can get with my lungs feeling like they're on fire — and shakily get to my feet. I grab the small trash can in the room and start picking up the larger pieces of glass, counting them and trying to calm myself down.

Once I pick up all the large shards, I walk over to my bed and press the call button. A nurse walks in with a bright smile on her face before she sees the mess on the floor.

"Oh, no!" She eyes the glass.

"Sorry." My cheeks are super-heated. "I overreacted. I'll pay for everything and clean up the mess I've made. I was just wondering where I could find a broom and dustpan."

"The cleaning staff can get it." She pulls out her phone and appears to be typing a message.

"No. Please. I made the mess, and I should be the one to clean it. Please, just have someone bring the broom and dustpan?"

She studies me for a moment before nodding and sending another message. Moments later, a man walks in with a broom and dustpan. I take them both and get to work cleaning up the tiny shards.

After finishing, I grab my phone. The first call I make is to Coach. There's no way to avoid telling him what's happening anymore. My hands shake the entire time I'm talking to him. I can hear the disappointment and sadness in his voice even as he tells me to get better.

The moment I'm off the phone with him, I scroll through my contacts and hover over Shane's number. I want to call him and tell him everything. He's the only friend I have who knows what I'm going through. I take a deep breath and dial his number, waiting as the phone rings.

"Hey, West." He sounds exhausted and I wonder if he's been up all night like I've been.

"I'm in the hospital."

The silence between the phone lines is loud.

"How bad is it?" Shane's voice cracks. "Be honest with me, West."

"Stage-four liver failure."

Shane sighs. "I'll be there soon."

"Tell me, Shane."

"You've got one life to live, so make it your mission to live it to the fullest." I can hear the tears in his voice and I am gutted. "I paraphrased one of my top ten favorite books, *Me Before You*." I can hear the sounds of his shallow, rapid breaths over the phone. "Baby, you're going to survive this, okay?"

He called me baby and I love it.

Nodding, despite knowing he can't see me, I say, "Will you stay on the phone with me until you get here? I don't want to be alone right now, but I can't handle my mom's crying."

"I'll stay on the phone as long as you need me to."

The room around me gets a little bigger and some of the pressure eases in my chest as Shane talks to me about anything that comes to his mind.

Chapter 17

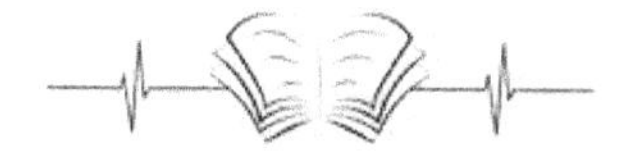

Shane

When I walk into West's room, I have a bag filled with junk food and DVDs. He looks up at me, a small smile on his handsome face, but I'm stunned by the yellow tinge to his skin. He didn't have the yellow tint yesterday.

"You look like shit," I say dryly as I drop the bag onto the chair in the corner and pull out a stack of movies. "I brought every shitty football movie I could find."

"You didn't have to do that." He shuffles over on his bed and makes room for me to sit down on the edge next to him. "They've got some pretty shitty cable here."

"And that's why I brought the movies." I sit and kick off my shoes. "I expected you to still be parading around in the hospital gown."

West laughs and looks down at his joggers and t-shirt. "As soon as I could get out of that damn thing, I changed."

"How are you holding up?" I look at the wires and tubes running from him to various machines and bags of fluid. "Looks like you're being loaded down with drugs."

"Something like that. I didn't pay much attention while they were hooking it up. There's supposed to be some sort of specialist coming who'll tell me more about my death sentence. So, naturally, I can't wait for that tomorrow. As if Mondays could get any better."

"I'll stay with you. Seems like you could use some company for the shit-fest that's about to happen."

West's eyes widen as he looks at me. "You don't have to do that."

"Doesn't matter. Let's watch one of these movies and eat bags of chips until we feel like throwing up."

West laughs and nods. He's quiet as the movie begins. As much as I want to pay attention to the actors on the screen, I can't. I'm focused solely on him.

I watch the way his eyes dart to the machine when he thinks I'm not watching him. He wrings his hands together before fisting them in the material of his joggers as if he has all kinds of energy built up and nowhere to expend it.

For the first time since we've met, I look at him and I see how weak he really is. I notice the weight he's lost and the dark circles beneath his eyes. His cheeks are hollowed out and when his hands aren't doing anything, they're shaking.

I don't know how to ease his fears or comfort him. But, god, I want to.

I can only imagine what he's feeling. Everything that happens next is entirely out of his control. He can't choose whether he lives or dies.

My stomach is twisting as one movie ends and I start another one. West runs a hand through his hair as I sit back down and lean into the pillows beside him.

"Coach knows what's happening. He's going to tell the rest of the team I have to step back from playing and attend to personal matters." West sighs and starts toying with the hospital bracelet around his wrist. "Please don't tell anyone what's actually happening to me. I don't want them to know."

"West, don't you think it's time you start letting your friends in?"

"My mom nearly had a breakdown during all the testing. Dr. Sullivan came in and told her I have stage-four liver failure and it was like the world had fallen out from under her feet."

"Can you blame her? She loves you. You're her son."

"I don't want her to spend however long I have left crying and thinking about death. I want to live like none of this is happening."

"Well, it's happening, and it's time you stopped running away from it."

West sighs and leans back, looking up at the ceiling. "Can we talk about something else? Literally anything."

"I was hauled into the dean's office today. Apparently, my attendance record is less than stellar and it's going to land me in more trouble with the disciplinary committee."

"The disciplinary committee?" The corner of his mouth curves up into a smile.

"I'm in some deep shit." I reach for the remote and turn the volume down on the television.

"Why is this the first that I'm hearing of it?" Interest lights up his face.

"I told you I needed you to talk to the dean and explain everything the day after...you know what," I tease. "You're the one who didn't listen when I told you I was in trouble with him."

"And why does the dean have such a hard-on for getting you in trouble?"

I shrug, knowing it's easier not to get into the politics of my family. "My uncle has always been kind of an ass. Well, more than kind of. He and my mom were always at each other's throats growing up. He's spent his entire life trying to prove he's better than everyone around him."

"The dean is your uncle? No fucking way." West starts laughing and shaking his head. "I've met the man, and holy hell, I wouldn't want to be related to him, either."

I shrug. "He saved my ass, which means I have to put up with him."

"How did he do that?"

"There was a rumor going around that I forged my SAT scores. It went to one of the education boards and instead of going to Yale like I had always planned, I was told I wouldn't be admitted to any university. They said that they had proof I forged the scores."

"So, if this is just your first year of college, how are you doing the same courses that I am? I'm nearly three years older than you."

"When your mom is dying in a hospital over the summer, you have a lot of time to consume information. And I started college courses in my junior year of high school and continued through my senior year. Plus, I was able to take the last of the credits for my second year over the summer."

"There's no way you had enough time for that," West says, his eyes widening as a nurse walks into the room.

"Time to get you settled for the night," the nurse says, as she approaches West to disconnect some of the meds flowing into him.

Once all the wires and tubes have been removed, the nurse leaves, closing the door behind her, and West rolls over onto his side to face me. He tucks one arm under his head and yawns.

"So, you finished two years of college while balancing your high school course load?"

"I told you; I didn't have much else to do besides comfort my mom when she needed me, making sure she knew I was there, even up until her dying breath. It was the least I could do for the amazing woman, the amazing mother, she was." I can feel the tears stinging the back of my eyes.

"And they still think you forged your test scores even after proving you can do all the work of both a high school and college student combined?"

I'm happy West doesn't think for a moment that I'm capable of being dishonest. It's nice to have someone in my life who doesn't automatically think I'm some kind of cheater who is willing to falsify scores to get ahead.

"Nope. They still insist they have proof, and I have no clue how that's possible." I still don't know how the disciplinary committee could have proof of something that never happened.

"Is being here going to get you in more trouble?" West asks.

"Doesn't matter. Being with you is more important." I roll onto my side to look at him.

"You mean that, don't you?"

"Why wouldn't I?"

"I'm terrified," he whispers, his eyes shining. "I'm going to die. There's no way they're going to be able to get me a new liver this quickly. I've been feeling like shit for days and I should have come to the doctor sooner, but I'm so fucking scared of dying."

"It's okay, baby," I whisper as I pull him into a hug, nuzzling my face into his hair. "I'm here for you."

For a moment, his body stiffens. I'm about to pull away when he tilts his head back. He's staring at me and I can feel my heart threatening to beat its way out of my chest as his lips find mine.

The kiss is hesitant at first, like there's something still holding him back. I don't want to push too far and scare him away. Instead, I draw back and look at him, searching his expression for something that says I'm taking advantage of him so I can force myself to walk away.

"I don't want to die with any regrets." He slides closer to me until his body presses against mine.

His touch is hesitant as his hand skates beneath my shirt. My nerves feel as if they've been lit on fire as his fingers trail along the planes of my stomach.

"West."

"Shane."

His lips are back on mine and my world is spinning out of control as he nips at my bottom lip. I moan low in my throat, pressing myself closer to him. I can feel the bulge in his pants, and it only makes me harder. His hand stills beneath my shirt, but his mouth is still moving against mine, our tongues moving together in tandem.

West presses himself against me harder, rubbing and thrusting, as his hand tightens on my hip. I roll us, straddling him and kissing my way down his jaw to his neck. He moans as his hips buck beneath me. West's hands grip the hem of my shirt. I sit up and pull it off over my head, not missing the way his eyes trail down my body.

He reaches up, his fingers weaving through my hair as he pulls me back to him. I moan as he pulls my hair lightly while nibbling on my lip. West moves quickly, flipping us over. He's between my legs, kissing his way down my torso. I grunt and clasp onto his shoulders as he bites at the skin just above my waistband.

One moment I think he's about to flick open the button of my jeans and the next he's gone, racing for the bathroom. I hear retching seconds after the door slams shut behind him.

With a groan, I get out of bed and look at the couch near the chair in the corner. It's not big enough for me to get comfortable on, but it's going to have to be good enough for the night.

By the time West stumbles back out of the bathroom and to his bed, I've found an extra blanket and some pillows in one of the cupboards. He doesn't say anything as he falls into bed and neither do I. This day has been long enough. We don't need to talk things out right now.

Despite what happened, I know it doesn't mean anything to West. He's still working on figuring out who he is, on top of the emotional stress of his diagnosis. The make-out session could have all been a drug-induced moment, or West just seeking physical comfort, or even plain old wishful thinking on my part.

But the tingle of my swollen lips contradicts the lie I tell myself.

There isn't a chance in hell I'll be able to unpack all of this tonight.

And I still don't know what I'm doing or why the hell I'm falling in love with a potentially straight man...who may be dying.

Chapter 18

West

I stare at Shane as he wakes up from another night spent on the couch in the hospital. He only leaves for school and then comes back in the evenings. It's been the same routine for the last three days. And we've gotten to know so much about each other during that time. I curse myself for having wasted so much time being his enemy instead of his friend in the early days.

"Morning," Shane says as he stands and stretches his lithe body. "That couch never gets any more comfortable."

"As happy as I am having you here with me, you don't have to stay, you know?" I feel guilty he's spending his nights with me rather than living his life. "You have other things to do and friends you haven't seen in days."

Shane shoots me a sharp look. "Shut the hell up. I'm not leaving you here alone all night to spiral out of control."

"One of my parents could stay."

"They're here during the day with you. I'm sure that's more than enough to drive you insane. If your mom says one more thing about how tight my pants are, I might scream."

I laugh and sit up straighter in bed. "You love the attention."

Shane shrugs and runs a hand through his hair. As I watch him, I wish my hands were the ones running through his hair. I don't know how far we would have gone the other night if I hadn't had to throw up.

Kissing him was an impulsive move, but it felt right. I want to do it again. Somewhere outside of the hospital where we can pretend we're just two people exploring their attraction toward each other.

"I've got to get going if I want to make it to class on time. You're still okay with me taking your car, right?"

My mom had driven Shane to pick up my car a couple of days ago. Since then, he's been using it to get back and forth between campus and the hospital.

"Yeah, take it. I'm not sure how much more of this I can put up with, though. I'm tired of staying trapped in this fucking room and being jabbed with needles."

"There's not a lot we can do about that right now, West. You're exactly where you need to be. If you start running all over town, what happens if you pass out somewhere again?"

"I don't know, but I'm tired, Shane. This is no way to spend the rest of my life, *if* it is the rest of my life. I want to get out of here for a few hours and pretend I'm not sick."

"You've been running around for months pretending you're not sick. I think now is the time to admit that you really are."

"There are things I haven't done that I want to do before I die."

"Like what?" Shane asks as he pulls on his shoes.

He's avoiding looking me in the eye. I know talking about dying upsets him.

I look down at my hands as my heart pounds in my chest. "I want to go on a date with a man and figure out who the fuck I am. Dying without knowing seems like unfinished business."

Shane sighs and grabs his backpack from the ground, slinging it over his shoulder as he heads for the door. Worry eats at me as he gets ready to leave. I don't know if he has anything to say to that and even if he does, I'm worried about what the answer might be.

Does he know he's the man I want to go on a date with?

"Tell you what," he says before he walks out. "Discharge yourself. It should take a few hours. I'll come back after I'm done with classes for the day."

"You're breaking me out?" I ask with a smile, not wanting to feel too hopeful.

"Yes, dude, I'm breaking you out. Just wear something warm and if anyone asks, this was all your idea."

As Shane leaves for the day, I feel the excitement bubbling to the surface. One of the nurses walks into the room shortly after Shane's left to check my vitals.

"I want to discharge myself." I sit straighter in the bed. "I feel fine and I want to go home."

"That's against the doctor's recommendation." She studies the chart at the foot of my bed. "If you leave, you'll have to sign waivers stating you know the risks of leaving against the doctor's orders, but you are choosing to do it anyway."

"I'll sign whatever you need signed. I just want to go home."

The nurse studies me for a moment before nodding and putting my chart down. "Alright, I'll let the doctor know. It will take a few hours for them to go over all the necessary paperwork with you."

"That's fine. I have time. I just want to get out of here."

She nods before leaving my room. I don't care how long it takes them to get the paperwork ready. I'll admit myself again in the morning, but for tonight, I just want one night of freedom. One last night to pretend like I'm not about to feel the worst I've ever felt. I know it's only going to get worse from here on out, but I don't want my last night of feeling good to be spent sitting in a hospital bed and waiting for more tests to be run.

I want to spend my last night as a normal person with Shane.

***

By the time I manage to discharge myself from the hospital, Shane is done with his classes for the day and back in town. He's sitting behind the wheel of my car, drumming his fingers to the beat of a song.

"Waiting on me?" I get in on the passenger's side.

"Might be. How do you feel about camping?"

"I haven't really done much of it. Neither of my parents was really the camping type. They preferred to be at home with their noses in books."

"My mom was like that too most of the time," Shane says as he pulls away from the curb. "She liked camping, though. My grandparents did too. At least once every summer we would pack everything up and then go camping for a week in the middle of nowhere."

"Listen," I say as he turns onto the highway. "I'm all for trying something new, but I'm not about to be shitting in a hole."

Shane laughs and looks at me. "There will be no shitting in holes. There are bathrooms on the campgrounds. You'll be fine."

"You know, I didn't think you were the camping type, either. You seem more like the type to sit at home and study."

"There's a lot you still don't know about me." Shane reaches for the volume and turns the music up.

I watch him as he drives, wondering how I've gone this long without ever really noticing him. He's right, there's a lot I don't know about him, but I want to get to know him. I want to know everything.

Shane doesn't say much. His eyes stay on the road, and he seems tense, as if there's something that's bothering him. I want to ask, but if he wanted me to know, he would have volunteered the information.

But I'm learning that I can't help myself when it comes to Shane. I've got to ask. "Are you okay?" I turn the music down and twist in my seat to take a better look at him.

"Fine." Shane sighs. "This is just a little weird, don't you think? We were barely friends two months ago and now we're — well, I don't know what the hell we are. Plus, you're really sick."

"I'm dying, Shane. It's okay to say that."

"There's still hope that you won't be. The doctors think there's a good chance of getting you a new liver. You'll be fine."

"Shane, I could die. There's no point in denying that. You know nothing good is going to come of pretending this didn't happen."

"I know." Shane glances over at me. His hands tighten on the wheel. "Still doesn't hurt to pretend for one night everything is fine. I thought that was the point of breaking you out of the hospital in the first place."

"It is. I don't want to talk about this anymore tonight, though. I'm tired of it. All we've talked about in the last few days is my condition. I'm exhausted."

"Fine." Shane reaches for the volume again. "We won't talk about it tonight. Just wait until I show you where we're camping."

"I'm going to like it?"

"You're going to love it."

***

After two hours of driving, Shane pulls off the highway onto a dirt road. He stops at a small building before coming back to the car with a parking pass. We drive another few minutes up a dirt road before he pulls into a spot that overlooks the most stunning waterfall I've ever seen.

"This is where we're staying?" I ask as he parks the car.

"This is where we're staying. Want to come help me set up camp or do you want to stay in here and relax while I do it?"

"I'm tired of sitting around and doing nothing. I want to help."

We work together to put up the tent and drag firewood over to the small fire pit. Shane shifts around a cooler of food, taking out a couple bottles of water before moving the cooler to the backseat of the car.

It doesn't take long to inflate the air mattresses and drag the sleeping bags into the tent. Shane tosses them into one corner while I grab the pillows and the heavy blankets from the back of the car.

Once the tent is set up, Shane starts a fire. He roasts hot dogs while I crack open a root beer and sit down on the top of the picnic table, dangling my legs over the side.

"This is a great view." I look out at the water crashing down on the lake below. "How did you find this place?"

Shane stands beside me and looks out over the water. There's a faint smile on his face, though his eyes are shining with tears he's trying to hold back.

"This used to be one of the spots Mom would take me camping. Last time we came here was a few months before she died. She had wanted one last trip before she was stuck in the hospital, too."

I don't think as I grab him and pull him to me. Shane's eyes widen as I cup his face, my thumb brushing over his cheekbone. I'd never thought of a man as beautiful before, but at this moment, Shane is the most beautiful person I've ever seen.

My hand moves to the back of his head, and I pull him closer. He stands between my legs and his gaze drifts down to my lips before he looks back up at me. He leans closer into me, his mouth finding mine as his hands move to my hips.

I bite at his bottom lip before my tongue darts into his mouth. Shane groans and presses himself impossibly closer.

I kiss him deeper. It feels like a fire has been lit between us and it threatens to consume me as his hands slip beneath my shirt. His fingers rake down my chest, his nails lightly scratching me and sending a shiver down my spine.

We kiss until everything around us fades away. No sickness or death is hanging over my head. There's just Shane and the feeling of his lips on mine. My body trembles as his teasing touch drifts over my skin.

His hands move down to my thighs, massaging them through my jeans. I'm stiff and straining against my fly as I tear my mouth away from his to trail kisses down his neck. Shane moans, his grip hard on my thighs as he pulls me to the very edge of the table. I grind against him, trying to relieve some of the tension that's building.

"We should stop." Shane pulls back, breathless. "I think I smell the hotdogs."

I laugh and sit back, noticing the scent of burned hotdogs filling the air. "I hope you brought more."

"I might have. I didn't know how much you'd eat, so I brought a lot."

Shane untangles himself from me and takes the charred hotdogs off the rack over the fire. He grabs another package of hotdogs from the cooler and places them on the rack.

As I watch him, I wonder what it would be like to wake up every morning to him preparing our meals while I look on, or vice versa.

"Shane, I think I'm bisexual," I say as he takes out a package of buns. "I really like kissing you, but I don't think I'm gay. I've had sex with women, and I enjoy it."

He looks over at me and shrugs. "Okay. You can use whatever label you want. It doesn't matter to me."

"You don't care that I'm not gay?"

Shane walks over to me and stands between my legs again. He reaches up, cupping my face. His thumb drifts over my jawbone as he looks at me.

"I like you whether you're gay or not."

"I like you too."

Shane's smile makes my heart skip a beat. I want to kiss him again, but he steps away and heads back to the food, turning the hotdogs over before they have a chance to burn again. My stomach growls as I join him by the fire.

If this is the way I get to spend my last night of freedom, I'm happy it's with him.

Chapter 19

West

When I open my eyes the next morning, Shane is awake and staring at me. He doesn't say anything as I leave my air mattress and move over to his. I have to admit, I'm a bit hesitant since I have no clue what I'm doing but I want to do everything. I don't want to die without having experienced what it's like to be with him fully.

I slide under his blanket and lean over him and his gaze drifts down to my mouth. I move slowly, my lips barely grazing his before I pull back slightly.

"You know," I say, my lips brushing against his as I speak, "there's something about being out here that lifts the weight off. There's nobody around to judge me for kissing a man and liking it. Nobody is going to say anything about me trying to figure out what I want in a partner."

"And what do you want?" Shane holds his breath as I push aside the blankets.

Out here, I feel bolder. I feel free and content in my attraction — in my feelings — for Shane.

I straddle his hips, rocking against the erection that's already forming. He groans as I lean down to kiss his neck. Shane moves quickly, his mouth finding my neck as his fingers weave through my hair. His teeth scrape against my skin, sending a shudder through me and an ache straight to my cock.

"Fuck," I hiss as his hands work beneath my shirt.

He grabs me by the hips and pulls me down harder, moaning as I grind against him.

"Are you sure?" Shane asks as I grab the hem of his shirt and start to tug it up. "We don't have to go any further than you want to."

"Can we just see where this goes?" I ask as he sits up slightly so I can pull his shirt off. "I don't want to put pressure on us by deciding what's happening right now. I just want to live in the moment."

Shane swallows hard and nods.

I sit back on my heels and look down at him. My tongue darts out to lick my lips as my hands smooth over his flat stomach, up to his chest. I lean closer to him, my mouth back on his neck. I nip and suck my way down his torso. He inhales sharply as I lick one of his nipples and then the other. He bucks beneath me, his fingers digging into my hips as his cock strains harder against his boxer briefs.

"Fuck, West."

I look up at him long enough to give him a playful smile before I lean down and take the other nipple into my mouth. Shane pants and whimpers as I lick and suck my way back up to his mouth.

My eyes widen as he suddenly flips us over. I breathe heavily as Shane kneels between my legs, looking down at me with reverence. My tongue darts out to lick my bottom lip as he reaches for my shirt. I help him get it over my head before falling back against the pillows.

Shane trails his hands down my stomach, reaching for my joggers. My cock is hard and straining against the fabric. It twitches as Shane runs a finger gently down it before leaning over to kiss and nip along my waistline. I moan and writhe beneath him as he rubs my cock through my pants.

My fingers tangle in Shane's hair, pulling his head back until he's looking at me. His hand stills on my cock as he stares at me.

"Want to stop?" Shane asks, hovering over me. "We can stop if you want."

"The only thing I want..." I release a nervous breath. "Is to fuck you."

Shane's eyebrows raise. I know my words must have shocked him, and he's probably thinking I'll change my mind and tell him I don't want him. But when my intense gaze doesn't waver, he swallows hard. I try to push down some of the lust that's surging through my body. This is my first time with a man, and I have no idea what to expect. There's a part of me that's terrified but the larger part is excited. If I'm going to sleep with any man, I want it to be Shane.

"West, are you sure that's a good idea? I don't want you to think you have to do this. Spending time with you is enough."

He's giving me an out, and I love him for it.

Oh, fuck!

Love?

That's an emotion I need to unpack later, but right now, my focus is on what I'm craving to do to Shane.

"And I said I want to fuck you." Confidence is evident in my voice. "I don't want any regrets, remember?"

"You can tell me to stop at any point and we'll stop." Shane kneels as he reaches into his backpack and takes out a bottle of lube and a couple condoms.

"So," I say with a smile as I glance at the lube. "You thought this would happen?"

Shane shakes his head but doesn't look like he can help the smile that lights up his face. "I didn't think this would happen, but I hoped you might be interested in exploring something sometime soon."

I sit up and kiss him again. We fall back into the bedding, our limbs wrapping around each other. His tongue slides against mine as the walls that have been built between us finally fall.

There's a sharp intake of breath as Shane pulls my joggers down. My cock bobs free, slapping my lower stomach, precum beading from the slit as Shane sits back to take in the view. For a moment, I want to pull the blankets over my body and hide myself from him, but those thoughts disappear when I see the way he's looking at me.

Shane wraps his hand around my cock, stroking as he sucks my head into his mouth. He works his hand up and down my length at the same time. I moan, my hips bucking off the bed as I drive myself deeper into his mouth. I've had blow jobs before, but nothing has ever felt as good as this. My hands fist in the sheet as he swirls his tongue around my cock.

Moaning, he works me deeper into his mouth, reaching up to play with my nipples while sucking hard. My hand grips the back of his head as I groan, moving my hips in time with Shane's sucking.

"I'm going to come," I say, rolling my hips and trying to get my cock deeper down his throat.

Shane stops sucking and pulls away from me. "Nope. Not yet."

"Tease."

"Do you want to stop, or do you want to keep going? I'm negative and I'm on PrEP."

"I'm negative too. They tested us at the beginning of the season. Haven't been with anyone since before then. But I don't know what PrEP is."

"Just a medication that reduces the risk of getting HIV."

"Oh," I say, my cheeks warming as I realize how little I know about being with another man.

"Want to top or bottom?" His fingers trail along my abs and my muscles quiver under his touch. His distraction works, drawing me back into the moment and out of my own head.

I had never given it much thought, but I owe it to myself to know what it's like to fuck him. To have him moaning my name as I bring him to his release.

"Top."

Shane pulls his briefs down and off, his cock standing straight up toward his belly, red and glistening at the tip. He's a bit longer than me but just as thick, and I find myself salivating, wondering what he tastes like. He leans over, pushing our cocks together, and then spits in his hand and wraps it tightly around us both, stroking us slowly from root to tip. Fuck, the sight of us pressed together is so hot. I don't know why I never thought to do this before.

Shane bends down and kisses me as we pant and thrust into his fist. After a couple more strokes, he stops his hand and pulls his mouth away, looking down into my eyes. "I can get myself ready for you if that's what you want. I know it's kind of intimidating your first time, and I want you to be as comfortable as possible."

"I want to experience everything."

"If you want to stop at any time, tell me, okay?"

"On your knees." I reach for the lube.

Shane moves off, bending over for me, his ass in the air and his face resting on his arms. I pour some of the lube onto his hole. He jerks forward slightly as I massage the lube into him, working one finger slowly inside. Shane moans, his back arching as I ease my finger in and out of him.

"How does that feel?" I run my other hand down his spine and watch the trail of goosebumps that appear.

"Good," he says, moaning as I add another finger, teasing him slowly.

"I need to suck you." Lust fogs up my brain as I reach around him with my other hand and stroke his cock.

He moves quickly, turning over onto his back. I look down at his cock and back up to his face, his tongue darting out to lick his lips again as he looks up at me. He looks so wrecked and so beautiful. My lips trail down his torso as my fist wraps around his cock. Moaning, he rocks his hips, and I grin, knowing he's desperate for my touch.

I suck on the head of his cock, moving my mouth up and down as far as I can without gagging. My hand moves in time with my mouth as I work him over the way he did me. His hips buck as I graze his cock with my teeth, drawing a deep moan out of him. His taste is musky and so fucking sexy. My cock twitches, leaking more precum. Yeah, I could definitely get used to this.

Before he finishes in my mouth, he pulls me off and looks at me through half-lidded eyes.

I sit back on my heels, admiring the view for a moment before grabbing more lube. He groans as I push two fingers into him again. He arches against my fingers as I circle them, stretching him.

"One more," Shane says, panting, his eyes rolling back in his head.

I add a third finger, watching as my fingers move in and out of him, pushing him slowly to the edge.

Shane moans loudly as I remove my fingers and push my cock inside him gently, letting him get used to me before I'm fully seated inside him. I pant, my chest heaving, as he tightens around me, my fingers digging into the flesh of his hips. He wraps his legs around my waist, and after a few seconds of him getting used to me, I start to move.

He's so tight I think I'm going to finish right then and there, especially when I see his hand go to his own cock, stroking it in time with my thrusts.

He arches his back as I thrust harder and harder, chasing after my release. I lean forward as I fuck him, propping myself up on one arm and replacing his hand around his cock with mine, stroking in time with my thrusts.

Moments later, he's groaning louder than before as his body tenses and spasms. The sight of his cum shooting onto his stomach and chest triggers my own release, and I unload inside him.

When the haze of our orgasms begins to fade, I ease out of him slowly, gently. I grab a washcloth and a bottle of water, and ignoring his protest, I clean Shane off. Then I grab another washcloth and clean myself up. Shane remains silent, his eyes averted, and I'm worried that I've just ruined everything.

Was I bad at it? Did that suck for him? Should I have done something I didn't know to do?

"Are you okay? I didn't hurt you, did I?" My mind runs through every possible scenario.

"I'm fine. More than fine," he says with a laugh before he kisses me. "How are you?"

"I hope we'll be doing that again." I'm happy everything hasn't crashed and burned.

Still, I know when we get back to the hospital, everything is going to change once again. I'll be waiting for a new liver and wondering if I'm going to die before I tell the man I love how I feel about him.

Chapter 20

West

The thought of being at the hospital looms over me like an evil folk character waiting in the shadows to pounce on me when I least expect it. What happened between me and Shane earlier this morning keeps playing over and over again in my head. I know I'm going to be hooked up to machines and tested repeatedly until I either die or get a new liver.

I'm still glad I was able to spend time with Shane. Being with him only cemented the feelings I knew were growing for him. I want to tell him exactly how I feel — that I think I might be in love with him.

"Are you ready?" he asks as he looks up at the hospital sign. "I'm not going to go anywhere, okay? I'll be with you through every step of it."

"I know." I want to hug him, kiss him, and thank him for everything, but it's not enough considering everything he has done for me throughout the semester.

"Let's do this." Shane grabs my duffel bag full of my clothes and hoists it over his shoulder. After taking a deep breath, he leads the way into the hospital.

"Where have you been?" my mom asks as soon as I walk to the admissions counter. "I came here this morning with breakfast and the nurse tells me you discharged yourself yesterday! What's wrong with you, Weston? I can't believe this."

"I just needed a night to think everything over."

"And you!" She turns on Shane, pointing her finger in his direction. "I bet you orchestrated this entire thing! The nurses have told me how you've been staying in my son's room! They tell me you're here every night. I bet you're the one that convinced him to do something stupid like discharging himself in the middle of treatment!"

"Ma'am," Shane says, his voice tight and his hands curled into fists at his side. "I'm West's friend, but I didn't encourage him to do anything. He's a grown man who is capable of making his own choices."

"Don't you ma'am me! I know you convinced him to go with you! Weston isn't stupid! He would never do something so reckless with his life! I want you out of this hospital and banned from seeing him, now!"

Shane's face pales as he looks at me. His lips press together as he nods curtly. "Alright. Well, I don't want this to sound rude, ma'am, but I'm not going anywhere until your son asks me to. He needs a friend by his side while he's going through this."

Mom's face turns a bright shade of red as she takes a deep breath, ready to start into her next tirade.

"Enough, Mom." I brush past the two of them and walk to the counter. "I'm back and I'm ready to start treatment. Shane's the only friend who knows what I'm going through right now, so he's going to be staying here whether you like it or not. I don't care."

"Weston!"

"Enough!" my voice booms, even as I slam my hand down on the counter. "That's enough! I'm the patient, so I'm the one who gets a say in who is in the room with me or not!"

The entire room is looking at us, but I don't care. I'm tired of her trying to control my life and I can't put up with it any longer. I know she means well, but there has to be a point when she stops and backs off.

"Fine, Weston," she says, her eyes watering. "Have it your way."

Mom turns and runs out of the hospital, sniffling as she goes. The nurses look at me like I'm supposed to be ashamed of speaking to my mother that way. There's a small part of me that is, but the larger part is happy I stood up to her.

"Hello," I say to the nurse behind the counter, plastering on a bright smile. "I have stage-four liver failure, and I'd like to admit myself for treatment."

Shane snorts behind me, barely hiding his chuckle.

The nurse grabs a stack of paperwork and a pen, placing them both in front of me. I get to work scrawling my signature and personal information, wishing I had one more night outside the hospital.

Mom walks back in and stands beside me, her spine stiff as she looks back at Shane. She rolls her eyes before looking at the paperwork and pointing to a place where I've made a mistake. I fix it and continue through the paperwork, but as I do, my head starts spinning.

My eyelids feel heavy, and the ground seems both far away and impossibly close. I hear people shouting and hands grabbing for me before my world goes black.

***

When I wake up, I'm back in the same private room. My mom is sitting in the chair in the corner and my bag is sitting on the couch. Everything is slightly blurry as I look around the room, trying to find Shane. He should be here, but I can't see him.

"Mom, where's Shane?" I squint as I try to clear my vision. I'm not seeing him at all. "He said he wasn't going to leave. Where is he?"

"We had that boy banned from your room," Dad says as he strolls in with two cups of coffee. He hands one to Mom before sitting down on the couch. "He's only bringing more stress into your life, and you need to focus on healing right now."

I feel like screaming. I want to tell them he's more than just my friend, but I don't know how. I'm not ready to have that conversation with them yet. I just want Shane to sit beside me and watch horrible football movies with me. I want him to walk into my room and tell me that everything's going to be awful, but he'll be here with me through it all. I want him to fill me in with quotes he's reading from his favorite books.

"He's my friend. I want him here with me. I don't want to go through this alone."

"You're not alone." Mom gets up and moves to sit on the end of my bed. "We're going to be here with you as much as we can."

I blink away the tears as I stare at her. "The same way you've been there for me when I tell you about my football games? The same way you show up to every important event for me? Or the same way you only have breakfast with me every Sunday so you can tell your friends how perfect your fucked up relationship with your son is?"

Mom's eyes shine with tears as she stares at me. "How can you say that?"

"How can you sit there and pretend it isn't true? Shane is yet another thing, something real, that's important to me, and you're rejecting him the same way you reject my playing football."

"Weston, do not speak to your mother that way," Dad says as he stands up and wraps his arm around Mom's shoulders. “I understand you’re stressed and scared, but that’s no way to talk to her.”

“You know what? You’re right.” I just want some peace and quiet. “I need some time to process all of this. Do you mind leaving me alone for a few hours? You can go get some food. It’s not like I’m going anywhere.”

“How can I believe that when you discharged yourself last night to take off with that man?”

“*That man* is my best friend. And since you’ve somehow managed to override your adult son’s wishes and had him banned, I’d like to be alone now.”

“Let’s go,” Dad says as he drops his arm from around Mom and heads to the door. “It’s clear he doesn’t want us here right now. Let’s give him the space he wants and then maybe in a few hours when we come back, he’ll finally understand how easy we’ve made life for him and how appreciative he should be.”

Mom sniffles and gets up, following Dad out of the room and slamming the door behind her. The second they’re gone, I slump back against the pillows. My head is pounding, and the room feels like it’s closing in around me.

I get up and search through my bag until I find my phone. I call Shane, but he doesn’t answer. With a sigh, I try calling him again, wondering how much damage my mother has done. The call goes to voicemail again. My heart is racing as I dial his number again.

“Shane, I don’t know what she said to you, but it probably isn’t true. Please, just call me back. I need you here. I’m scared shitless and I don't know how the fuck I'm going to get through this without you."

I hang up and try calling him again. When it goes to voicemail for the fourth time, I throw my phone back onto the couch and shuffle back to my bed.

The room is suffocating as I fall back on the bed and stare at the ceiling. I feel weak, as if my bones are made of jelly. Exhaustion flows through my body and I want to sleep, but worrying about Shane is keeping me awake.

Where is he? Why didn't he stay?

"Hey there, honey," a nurse says as she opens the door and walks into the room. Another nurse trails in behind her with more equipment. "It's time to get you attached to some machines for monitoring and medication."

"Great," I mutter, taking a deep breath before sitting up. "Stick me with as many needles as you want, it's not going to make me feel any better."

"That's the attitude," the nurse says with a laugh as she and the other nurse start setting everything up.

"Do you mind passing me my phone?" I ask, pointing at the phone on the couch.

"Not at all."

She grabs the phone and hands it to me before starting to hook me up to all the machines. I sigh as they work, wanting to disappear into oblivion.

CHAPTER 21

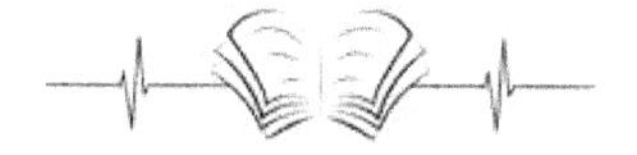

Shane

I never thought anybody could be such a piece of work until I met West's mother. I could see why she blamed me for his leaving the hospital. After all, I had driven the getaway car and encouraged him to live one last night of normalcy. When he passed out, I was the one who caught him. We had both gone tumbling to the ground and my head smacked hard against the ground. One of the nurses had insisted I see a doctor.

Unfortunately, that meant sitting for several hours and wasting the rest of the day in the emergency room. While I was there, I tried to call West a couple times but there was no signal. By the time I got his messages, he was already asleep for the night and I had to head back to campus for class the next morning.

Twenty-four hours later, I'm waiting until his mom and dad leave his room. The moment they do, I pace by the door, peeking inside to see if West is awake. When I hear his soft snores, I keep moving to the little waiting area and take a seat. I don't want to wake him up when I know that he isn't getting much rest.

I stretch my legs out in front of me and open my textbook. Even if I'm not at school when I should be, I can at least get some of my work done. Uncle James knows where I am and why. While he isn't happy I'm missing more school, he did agree to intervene with the disciplinary committee and explain that I'm away to be with a friend who's hospitalized.

When I talked to him about West, I left out the way I feel for him. I'm not ready to have that conversation on the off chance that the worst happens. Having someone else know how I feel about him would only make grieving him that much harder.

Instead, I lose myself in the world of economics, trying not to remember how it was when my mom was dying. I'd buried myself in books, whether they were for me to study from or for me to derive a few hours of pleasure. It all feels too similar and the old feelings have started to rush back.

My chest tightens as I glance up at West's room, wishing I could be in there with him. While one of the nurses has taken pity on me, she's already said she's pretending she doesn't know me if his mom catches me hanging around.

The waiting area is busy with people moving back and forth between room to chair and back again. I wonder if their loved ones are terminal or if they're only here for a short time. I wish I had someone else to sit with, to keep me company.

When I'm with West, it's easy to pretend everything is going to be fine. I say it enough times to him, I can almost convince myself it's true. I can imagine everything really is going to be alright because it's easier to tell him than it is to tell myself.

Right now, trying to convince myself he's going to make it feels like a lie. It feels like I'm getting ready to rip my own heart out and light it on fire because I know nothing is going to be alright. The doctors are in a race against time to find him a liver, and I don't think they're going to win.

West's mom abruptly appears before me, her lips pressed together and her hands on her hips. I wait, holding my breath, as she opens her mouth and then closes it. She sighs and slumps into the chair beside me.

I close my textbook, trying to prepare myself for the worst.

"I love my son, despite what he may say sometimes. His dad and I have never known how to connect with him, but I love him. His brother and sister love him too, even though they're not around anymore."

"I don't doubt that you love him." I put my textbook into my backpack.

"He hasn't talked about you much, but I'm willing to guess you're someone special to him. He's brought girlfriends home before and I liked most of them, but he never looked at them the way he looks at you."

The room feels like it's a thousand degrees and I would do anything to not be having this conversation right now. A lump rises in my throat as I stare at the floor, trying to forget that the way he looks at me is something special.

Suddenly, the hallway is filled with an electronic scream. I hear doctors and nurses yelling about a crash cart but they go racing by before turning sharply and entering West's room. His mother is on her feet and racing after the nurses. Her screams are shrill and send a shiver down my spine.

I tremble with fear, wanting to get up and follow them, but I know that his mother doesn't want me anywhere near his room. The fact that she didn't call security when she saw me in the waiting area was enough of a surprise.

"My baby!" his mom screams as two nurses wrestle her outside the room.

"I've got her." I rise to my feet and race across the hall to help them.

West's mom collapses in my arms as I haul her away from the room and back to the waiting area. She cries into my shoulder, her tears soaking my shirt as I hold her tight. I can hear the sound of the crash cart and the nurses counting compressions as they try to get West's heart going again.

"You know," she says with a sniffle as she pulls away from me and sits down. "I'm not a match. Neither is his dad. His brother and sister came into town for testing too and neither of them match. I don't know what we're going to do. They say that a match might become available on the list soon, but there's no way of knowing."

"I know," I whisper as I stare at the room. My heart is caught in my throat, my knees are like noodles, and I feel like any time soon, I'll collapse and cry.

"Please save my baby boy." West's mother moans, as the door to West's room slams shut. "Please save my baby."

Time seems to stretch into eternity as she takes my hand and squeezes it tight, holding it like it's the only thing tethering her to this world. We wait together, staring at the closed door and waiting for it to open again. This can't be the end. It can't be.

What feels like hours later — but is probably only forty-five minutes — the door slowly opens, and the crash cart is wheeled out, followed by several nurses. Another nurse steps out of the room and scans the waiting area. When she and West's mother make eye contact, West's mom gets up and heads into the room, leaving me waiting for whatever happens next.

***

West's mom doesn't come out of the room for the rest of the night. I take it as a good sign that he is still alive. Still, it doesn't stop me from sleeping in the waiting area and hoping I get a chance to see him.

When I wake up in the morning, doctors are still coming and going from West's room. Nurses dash in and out, concerned looks on their faces as they shake their heads at each other.

My stomach plummets to my feet as I watch their exchanges, wondering what is going on. Even after last night, West's mom still has me banned from her son's room. It doesn't matter though; it looks like everyone is being banned from his room. His mom and dad wait outside, staring in through the window in the hallway as a team of doctors closes the door and surrounds West's bed.

"What's happening in there?" I ask a nurse as she stops to check her phone. "Is West alright?"

The nurse looks me over. "I'm sorry. If you're not family, then I can't tell you anything about what's happening."

"Please." My vision blurs. I'll beg her to tell me if that's what it takes. I need to know what's happening to West. "Please. He's my best friend. If he's not going to make it, I need to know."

"He's not doing well. We're hoping for the best, but we're running more tests to see what's happening in his body."

"Is there a transplant scheduled yet?"

"I can't give you that much information," she says as her phone starts ringing. "You seem like you care a lot about him. The best advice I can give you now is to cross your fingers and hope for the best."

I nod and walk away from her. The room is closing in around me and I want to scream. There's nothing I can do to help him. The last time I felt this helpless was when my mother was dying. I don't know how I'm going to keep going if West dies too.

The doctors open the door after a while and walk away. West's mom and dad still stand at the hallway window. Both of them go in for a few minutes before coming back out and standing at the window again.

With a sigh, I pull out my phone and call West. I cross my fingers, hoping he answers. The phone rings forever but finally, the call connects.

"I tried calling you the other night." His voice is raspy and slow. "You didn't answer."

"I was in the emergency room. There's no signal there. Then when I came back upstairs, you were sleeping most of the day and night. And then there was the crash cart. Are you okay?"

"I'm not okay, Shane. Can you come in here?"

"West, you know your mom doesn't want me anywhere near you. As much as I want to, I don't want to make them angry with you right now. You don't need to be dealing with that kind of stress."

West sniffles before he clears his throat. "I understand. Just promise me you won't leave, okay? Can you at least come to the window?"

I look over at his parents who are still glued to the hallway window. "I can't. Your mom and I talked last night, and I think she knows about us, but she still didn't say I could be around you. I don't want to disrespect her."

"Give me five minutes," he says before hanging up.

I watch, holding my breath as West calls his parents back into his room. I walk over to the same spot where Mr. and Mrs. Perkins were standing and look into West's room. They are both talking to him. His mom hauls him into a tight hug before stepping back and nodding. I don't know what he said to his parents, but both of them leave the room and walk to the elevator bank. They didn't look my way, although they must have known as soon as they stepped out of West's room that I was standing there.

As they get onto the elevator, my phone starts ringing and West's name flashes across my screen.

Answering the call, I look through the window and study West. If it's possible, he looks like he's lost even more weight. There are dark circles under his eyes. His skin is more yellow than it was a few days ago.

"You look like shit," I say as I stare at him, wishing I could hold him and tell him that everything is going to be alright.

He chuckles lowly. "I feel like shit. Come inside and stay with me. Please, Shane."

Our gazes lock through the window. I nod and end the call before walking into his room and heading straight for him. I pull him into a tight hug, trying to hold back the tears as I kiss his forehead. His skin is scorching hot against my lips.

"Are you running a fever?"

"Yeah. They say my body has started attacking itself and the fever is a sign of that. It's fine."

"It's not fine," I say, tears tracking down my cheeks. "Do they have a transplant figured out for you yet?"

"No. My brother and sister aren't matches and neither are my parents. None of the people listed as donors have come back as a match or are willing to do it. Shane, this is going to be the end. It could be the last time I see you."

"No," I say, cupping his face. "This isn't the last time. It can't be the last time. We have so much left to figure out."

"I'm tired of fighting, Shane." He sighs and leans into my touch, his eyes closing. "I'm so fucking tired of fighting this off. I just want to rest."

I help him over to the bed and wait until he's settled before pulling the blankets back over him. "You get some sleep then. I'm not going anywhere. I'll be in the waiting area until I can come in here again, okay? Just don't die on me. Please don't die, baby."

"I don't think I have a choice anymore. Dr. Sullivan is still hopeful, but I can't tell if she's just saying that to make me feel better."

I lean down to kiss him, tasting the salt of our tears on our lips before I pull back. "I'll see you soon."

"Shane?"

"Yes?"

"I love it when you call me baby."

My lips curl into a smile. "I love to call you baby."

I turn to leave.

"Tell me, Shane."

I stop in my tracks, then swivel around.

With my gaze focused on him, I clear my throat. "I love you, West...always. Whether we win or lose this fight, I'll love you through it...and even after, I'll still be loving you."

I turn on my heel and leave the room. I'm full and overflowing with emotion. I wipe my eyes and look around. Four nurses are behind a desk, pouring over paperwork and answering phones. I approach one of them and try to slip on a polite smile, even though I feel like poison is running through my veins.

"Hi." I lean against the counter. "Can I talk to Dr. Sullivan, please?"

"One moment." I assume when the dark-haired nurse picks up the phone that she's calling the doctor. She turns away from me, speaking low before hanging up the phone and turning back around. "Follow me."

She leads me to another floor of the hospital before stopping in front of a glass door. Dr. Sullivan looks up as I enter.

"How can I help you?"

I sit down in a chair across from her and take a deep breath. "I need your help with something."

She nods and leans back in her chair. "Let's talk then."

Chapter 22

West

Exhaustion overtakes me, even after several hours of sleep. I've never been this tired before and if I make it through this, I never want to be this tired again. I yawn and shift in the bed, my body aching as I sit up. Mom is sitting in the corner with mascara tracks down her cheeks. Getting her to leave after my heart stopped has been nearly impossible. Even getting her to go away for a few minutes the night before so I could talk to Shane was like begging for rain in the middle of a drought.

"Morning," she says before taking a long sip of her coffee. I can see the cup shaking in her hands and I feel horrible. I didn't want to drag her into this. "Dad's gone to work, but I've taken some more time off."

"Anything new happen overnight?" My voice is raspy as I reach for the glass of water. I look out the window to the hallway and see Shane sitting in the waiting area. He looks up as if he can sense I'm watching him and winks. I can't help the smile that spreads across my face as I look back at my mom.

"You have a boyfriend," she says slowly. "I didn't see that coming."

"He's not my boyfriend." I fist the sheets in my hands. "I don't know what he is."

"Well, he's barely left your side in days, and I know the only reason you sent your dad and me away last night was to see him. He seems like a nice enough young man. I was wrong about him."

It feels as if a weight I didn't know I had been holding is lifted from my shoulders. Mom smiles and takes another sip of her coffee.

"I'm bisexual."

"Honey, I'll love you no matter who you love. Don't ever feel like you have to keep something like that from me again. I know I haven't been the easiest of mothers, but I'm going to do better."

"I love you too, Mom."

I know that the odds aren't good. I've been on the transplant list for weeks and nothing has come of it. There's no new liver walking through the door to save me.

This is the end and I'm stuck in the hospital.

"So," I say, switching the topic back to my original question, "has there been any news?"

"None. Dr. Sullivan came by earlier and said she would be by once you're awake."

I nod and run my hands down my face. "Alright. When are Thomas and Laurie coming?"

It's been a long time since I've seen my siblings. I know they're in town and have been tested, but they haven't been to my room yet.

"They said they'd come see you tonight. I'm holding them to that, but it's hard on both of them to see you this way. Laurie has been crying for days and Thomas has been drinking again."

"Great," I mutter, pinching the bridge of my nose. "Maybe it's better if they don't come by."

"They're going to come see you, Weston."

I hear the words she's not saying. Thomas and Laurie are going to come see me because this might be their last chance.

"Good morning!" Dr. Sullivan says as she sweeps into the room with a clipboard in her hand. "How's everybody feeling today?"

"Like shit," I say before taking another sip of my water. I set the glass on the table and lean back into the pillows. "Is there any update on the list?"

"I've been making all the calls that I can, and I've gotten you bumped nearly to the top. The fact that you're a young athlete is promising, but with your condition being incurable, it brings your position on the list back down by some. There are multiple factors that go into consideration for who gets a transplant or not, as I've explained to you previously."

"So, where do I sit on the list?" I ask, confusion coursing through my mind. "You said I'm at the top, but now I'm not, so what's going on?"

"You're still near the top," Dr. Sullivan clarifies as she looks down at her clipboard. "According to the notes I have received from my superiors, while you aren't their first dozen or so priorities, you're not far behind."

"Great," I say, wanting to scream. "So, there's only a dozen people before me waiting for a liver."

"I know it's hard," Dr. Sullivan says. "But you have to have hope."

"I know," I say. "Is there anybody on the donor list that might be a match?"

"We're still looking. I promise you I'm doing all that I can to make sure you get your liver. It's just taking a little more time than we had originally anticipated."

"I don't think I have much time left, Dr. Sullivan." I stare up at the ceiling. "I'm exhausted, and even breathing takes a lot of effort. The medications you keep pumping me full of aren't helping with the pain and I hate being here."

"I know." The doctor reaches out to squeeze my shoulder. "This isn't easy, especially when you are so young. We're going to keep working until we find you a donor though. I have several promising leads from donors on the other side of the country. It's just a waiting game now to see if they are in fact matches for you."

"And if they aren't?" Mom asks, her voice rising an octave above its normal pitch. "You keep telling us that you're working on finding him a donor, but all I've seen so far is the inability to find one. You keep telling us it looks promising and yet nothing has turned up yet. How are we supposed to believe you're doing all you can when no real progress has been made?"

Dr. Sullivan purses her lips, and a wrinkle appears between her eyebrows. "Mrs. Perkins, I assure you that my team is working as hard as they possibly can. I have the best liver specialist I know preparing to do the surgery and consulting as much as possible until he can arrive. Your son has met with him several times in the past to discuss what is happening."

"And yet, there's still nothing actually being done!" My mother's tone is sharp. "You say you're doing all you can and there's a specialist involved but my son is still very sick."

"I don't know what else you would like me to say, Mrs. Perkins. We've done all we can and now we must wait."

I sigh and run a hand down my face, wishing this was all over. I never asked to spend my life living like this. I don't want to lie in this bed and listen to them argue. My last moments alive can't be filled with listening to my mother fight with my doctor.

"I'm exhausted. Do you both mind taking this outside so I can get some more sleep, please?" I don't bother to open my eyes and look at them.

Once I hear the door shut behind them, I breathe a sigh of relief. The arguing was too much. I know my mom is worried, but Dr. Sullivan is doing all that she can. The rest is out of our hands.

There's a sort of peace that comes with accepting you can do nothing to change your fate.

Exhaustion washes over me in pounding waves. Even though my body is aching, I find it easy to let myself fall asleep again. After all, sleeping is easier than being awake and dealing with the reality of my impending death.

***

When I wake up, Mom is nowhere to be found, and it's dark outside. Thomas and Laurie are sitting on the couch and both of them look like they've seen better days.

"Well, look who finally woke up." Laurie gets to her feet and races over to the bed, pulling me into a tight hug. "I've missed you, baby brother. How could you go get sick like this and not tell us?"

I grin and hug her back, inhaling the scent of her vanilla-scented perfume. It's the same one she's worn for the last ten years, and I know I'm going to miss the smell when she leaves.

"I'm sorry, Laurie. I know you and Thomas have other things to do. I didn't want to burden you with my shit, too."

"I don't care what's happening in my life." Thomas approaches the bed and hugs me after Laurie steps aside. "You call me when something happens and I'll be on the next plane out here. You're our baby brother. Family has to stick together."

"Now," Laurie says as she sits on the end of my bed and crosses her legs, "tell us about how crazy Mom has been through everything. I can only imagine the ways she's been terrorizing the nursing staff."

"You wouldn't believe it." I launch into stories about Mom and the last several days at the hospital.

When I finally run out of stories and glance away from my siblings to see if Shane has taken up residency in the hall, I find him standing in my doorway with a DVD in hand.

"I went to the game tonight for you." Shane walks into the room. "I thought you might want to watch the last game of the semester."

After a quick, slightly awkward introduction between Shane and my siblings, Laurie announces, "We've got to get going," Laurie says, glancing at her watch. "Have a good night. I'll come see you again in the morning."

"Bye." I watch as they go.

Shane closes the door behind him. All it takes is one look at him without anybody else around and the tears finally start rolling down my cheeks. Everything that's happening feels like the end, and I don't know what to do. It feels like everyone is waiting for me to die.

"It's going to be okay," Shane whispers. He climbs into the bed beside me.

His arms wrap around me, and I turn into a puddle of tears. Once the crying starts, I can't seem to make it stop. I take deep breaths, trying to calm myself down.

"Did you mean it, Shane?"

His eyebrows crinkle in confusion. "Mean what?"

"That you're in love with me, that you'll always love me."

His gaze softens on me. "I meant every single word. I love you, baby. I'm stupidly, completely in love with you."

My heart melts, melts into liquid fire. I love him too. I'm in love with him. But I don't want to tell him how I feel, only to die, and our love never gets the chance that it deserves.

He's a sensitive man, and he's probably doubting if I have any feelings for him, like he does for me. I want to reassure him that I do, but what if I tell him, and he's happy to hear the words, only to be mired with sadness because I died?

Shane's hand drifts up and down my back, trying to soothe me. There's no solace in what's happening to me. I didn't do anything to make myself get sick. I'm too young to die, but my body doesn't seem to care about that. If there was something I had done that brought this on, or if there was something I could do about it, being sick might be more manageable.

Instead, it's all out of my control. There's not a single thing I can control about my situation.

"It's going to be okay," Shane says, his voice soft as he holds me tight, his hand still drifting along my spine. "It's going to be okay. We're going to figure this out."

"I don't know how we're going to figure this out." I lean into his shoulder as my tears finally slow down. My eyes ache from crying and the minuscule amount of energy I had drains from my body.

"I went to see Dr. Sullivan about getting tested. We'll find out in a couple of days if I'm a match for you or not. If I am, you're getting part of my liver."

I pull back to stare at him. It takes a few minutes to process what he's said. He's gone to the doctor to see if he's a match. He's willing to undergo massive surgery and lose a part of one of his organs for me.

"My mom didn't ask you to do that, right? It wouldn't surprise me if she did. I don't doubt she's off asking half of the hospital if they're registered donors and if they might not mind getting tested again just to make sure they aren't a match."

Shane laughs and pushes my hair back from my face. "No, your mom didn't ask me. Apart from the other night, she's still pretending I don't exist."

"She'll come around eventually." I'm not quite convinced that she will. "Are you sure that nobody asked you to do that?"

"Nobody asked me. If there's a chance to save you and I don't at least get tested, I'll hate myself for it. There's no way I would be able to live with that, baby."

"Shane, it's too much."

"West, being your potential donor, hopefully saving your life, is not nearly enough."

My eyes start watering again as I lean forward and kiss him. There's emotion behind the kiss that hasn't been there before, as if this could be our last. My hands thread through his soft hair, holding him close to me before we part.

It's dark in the room as we stare at each other, moonlight shining through the windows that overlook the hospital parking lot. My eyes close as exhaustion courses through my body again. I fall back into the pillows and stare up at the dim lights. Laurie had dimmed them a few hours ago after I complained about the headache starting.

"Shane, this all feels like one big nightmare I can't wake up from."

"It'll be over soon." He gets up and starts the recording of the football game. "It'll all be over soon, and then we can start living like normal people again. You'll get better."

"I'm going to be on medication for the rest of my life, even if I have a liver transplant."

"Being on medication is better than being dead." Shane settles in beside me again. He pulls the blankets over us and puts his arm around my shoulders.

I lean back into his embrace, trying to commit this moment to memory. Even if the time I have left is getting less and less, I never want to forget the feeling of being in Shane's arms while I fall head over heels for him.

Chapter 23

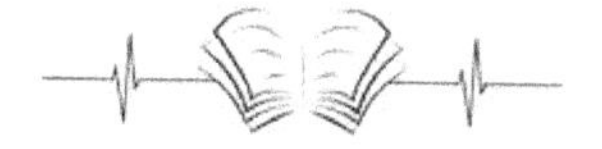

Shane

When I wake up a couple of mornings later, West is still asleep, though he looks like he hasn't slept at all. The circles beneath his eyes are darker than ever and his mouth hangs slack as he breathes shallow breaths. He's hardly been eating.

Not that I blame him. Even though I've only been seeing him at night after his parents and siblings have left, I can see how much eating makes him sick. Even when I bring slices of his favorite pizza, he can't keep them down for long.

"What are you staring at?" he mumbles as his eyes open slowly, squinting against the light as he rolls onto his back.

"You, I'm staring at you." I get out of the cramped hospital bed and stretch. "What do you say we load you into a wheelchair and go for a walk in the hospital's courtyard? It's been a couple of days since you got some fresh air."

West frowns and shakes his head. "I don't want you feeling like you have to stay here and take care of me. You've been here for three nights and you haven't left. Aren't you tired?"

"Ah," I say as I rummage through my backpack for a fresh change of clothes. "I see we're in one of our *'the world is going to end'* moods today. I have bad news for you, though. I'm not going to let you drag my mood down and ruin the day."

"Day is already ruined." He struggles to sit up. "I woke up and there's not a new liver in my body and the old one is trying really hard to kill me."

"Probably needs to try harder." I kiss his cheek before disappearing into the washroom for a shower.

After I shower and change, I head back into West's room and take a seat on the couch. West stares at the ceiling, swallowing hard. If the mood in the room was any worse, I'd think we were actually in hell.

I don't know what I can do to help him and it kills me. Dr. Sullivan said she would rush the testing, but it could also take a few days. A few days came and went, but she still hasn't given me an answer yet.

West is running out of hope — if that's even possible at this point. I thought he was at his lowest already, but it turns out I was wrong. West is a thousand times worse today than he was yesterday.

"I'm going to go find a wheelchair and then you can quit your bitching, bundle up, and get your ass outside for some fresh air."

"I'm afraid that will have to wait." Dr. Sullivan sweeps into the room with a clipboard in her hand. "I need to speak with you, Shane. Do you mind stepping into the hall?"

"Can we talk about it here?"

If it's bad news, I don't want to be the one to break it to West. My heart is too fragile to watch him break again. He's already falling into a million tiny pieces in front of me every time he wakes up.

"If you don't mind Weston knowing, then yes."

"I'm okay with that." I look at West and give him a small smile.

He crosses his arms, leaning back into his pillows. I can nearly hear the thoughts running through his mind. He thinks this is a waste of time. He's already talked to me late last night about pulling the wires and tubes keeping him alive, and just letting him live the rest of his life unattached to machines.

"Well, the tests have all come back positive for a match. Shane, you are the perfect candidate to donate to Weston," Dr. Sullivan says, a smile stretching across her face as she hands me the clipboard. "Everything looks good and if you're okay with it, I'd like to get started as soon as possible."

I grin and turn to look at West. Tears are rolling down his cheeks as a smile slowly spreads across his face. I want to run out of the room and shout the good news to the four corners of the world. I'm sure he feels the same way if the shaking of his hands is anything to go by.

There's a part of me that doesn't believe I could be a match. It has to be a cruel joke that someone's playing. The longer Dr. Sullivan's smile holds in place, the more real her news feels.

"Holy shit!" I say as I pull West into a tight hug. "You're getting a liver transplant!"

West laughs and wipes his eyes, hugging me back. His grip tightens around me before I step away and look back at the doctor.

"How soon?" I ask, thinking that right now wouldn't be soon enough.

"There are some procedures we have to go through, but two days from now, we could operate," the doctor says. She looks over to West with a wide smile. "You're getting a liver."

West looks at the doctor with wide eyes. "This isn't a joke, is it? There's no one waiting to wake me up from a dream, or to say it's all in my imagination?"

"No, nobody is going to tell you this is a prank," Dr. Sullivan says, grinning as she hands him the clipboard. "You're getting a liver, and this is all the pre-surgery paperwork you need to fill out."

West looks at the stack of papers and swallows hard. "Can I fill it out in a few hours? We're going to go outside and get some air."

"Absolutely. I just need them before seven tonight so I can get everything moving."

West nods and sets the paperwork to the side. "Okay. Thank you."

Dr. Sullivan leaves the room as quickly as she came. Once the door shuts behind her, West looks at me with wide eyes.

"Holy shit, did that just happen?" he asks.

"That just happened. You're getting a new liver."

"What if my body rejects it?" he whispers, running his hands down his face. "What if you go through major surgery and my body rejects it? You're going to hate me after going through all that for nothing."

"I could never hate you," I say, crossing the room and pulling him into a tight hug. "The surgery is worth even a chance at a life. If your body rejects the liver, well, at least we tried."

"How are you so calm about all this? I wish I was that calm."

"Both of us being worried about the surgeries isn't going to help anything. What we need is to take our minds off what's happening. Get bundled up and we'll go outside and play in the snow."

"I don't think I'm in any shape to play in the snow." West gets out of bed. He's shaky on his feet as he grabs the clothes I tossed on his nightstand the night before.

"You can watch me lick poles," I say with a wink, grinning when he laughs at the innuendo. It's the first time in weeks I've heard him laugh that hard. It warms me inside to know that even when he's feeling miserable, I can still make him laugh.

Once West is bundled up and disconnected from the machines, one of the nurses helps me get him outside. The air is chilly, but the sun tries to warm the earth below. Our breath blows out like clouds as we make our way along the paths of the courtyard.

West is quiet as I push him. He nestles deeper into the thick blankets wrapped around him, his cheeks and nose a rosy red. As we go down the twisting path, he tilts his head to look back at me.

"I hate this fucking wheelchair."

I squeeze his shoulder and smile. "You hate a lot of things right now, but I have a surprise for you, so try to be in a better mood."

We round another corner and I see the man I've been waiting for. Coach Veer is standing by one of the fountains, his hands stuffed deep in his pockets as he glances around the surrounding area. When he sees us, a bright smile lights up his face.

West shrinks back in the wheelchair, pulling the blankets even tighter around him. He looks at me with a scowl before looking back at his coach. I know he told the coach a little about his disease and hospitalization, but I doubt he told him everything that's going on and how bad it's gotten.

"Hello Coach," West says, his voice weak.

"Hello Perkins, how're you doing?" Coach Veer looks over West and sighs. "I wish you had told me more of what was happening. We would have figured something out for you earlier."

"It's really not something I wanted to talk about." West rubs the back of his neck. "It made it all too real if I started talking to people about it."

"We're your team, Weston, and the road to recovery is hard. You're going to need a support system now more than ever. Let your team be by your side through this process." Coach glances at me. "This young man clearly is. He came to me last night and told me what was happening."

West nods and looks back at me, offering me a small smile before he turns to the coach. "I know. I don't know how I'm going to tell the guys."

"When you're ready, we can tell them together." Coach reaches out to squeeze West's shoulder. "You're not in this alone. You have a whole team of people behind you, waiting to support you. And when you're ready to come back and the doctors have cleared you to play, your team will be ready and waiting for you."

"You're still going to let me play?" West's voice is hopeful and his eyes glisten as he looks at Coach. "I thought my football career would be over."

"I have some scouts who are very interested in you. After I'm done here, I have a meeting with two of them to explain what is happening. I won't go into the details, just that you are undergoing a medical procedure and require a few months off."

"Thank you, Coach," West says, sounding as if there's a lump stuck in his throat. "I appreciate that."

"Take care and get better." Coach Veer grins at West. "We're rooting for you."

West stares at the place where the coach stood long after he is gone. I consider wheeling him back into the hospital, but I don't want to go back in until he's ready. We don't know what's going to happen after surgery and he may as well enjoy the air while he can.

Eventually, he asks to go back inside. I wheel him back to his room where his mom is already waiting for him with a steaming cup of coffee in her hand. In the time that I've spent at the hospital, I've never seen his mom look more hopeless or tired. She's staring into the cup as if she doesn't know where she is.

"Mom? Are you okay?"

"Don't ask me that," she says softly, looking up at West. "You went outside?"

"Yeah, Dr. Sullivan brought some paperwork in for my liver transplant, and it looked like a lot to deal with all at once, so we went out to get some air."

Her eyes nearly pop out of her head as she stands up and squeals. She puts her coffee down before racing across the room to hug her son. I watch the exchange as they both tear up. I start to head for the door, wanting to leave them to have their moment. I'm sure they have a lot to talk about, especially once they start digging into the paperwork, and I don't want to intrude.

"Wait, Shane," West says, twisting around to grin at me. "Come back here."

"Are you sure?" I ask, cutting my gaze toward his mother.

"Mom, the liver donor is Shane. He got tested a few days ago, and it turns out he *is* a match."

His mom abandons him to pull me into a tight hug. At first, I stand there awkwardly, not knowing what I'm supposed to do. This is the closest she and I have been since West coded.

"Thank you for saving my son," she whispers, pulling back, tears in her eyes. "I know a thank you will never be enough. You don't know how much this means to me. My baby has a shot at life."

"Mom."

"Shush," she says with a grin. "I'm going to enjoy the moment. I'm going to go call the rest of the family and let them know the good news. Is there anything you want me to bring for dinner? I was craving a burger from that little place you love."

"We'll take a couple burgers," West says.

His mom nods and hugs him again before leaving the room to make her calls. As soon as she's gone, he slumps in the wheelchair and runs a hand down his face. I watch him get out of the wheelchair and shuffle back to the bed, staying a couple of steps behind him in case he starts to fall.

"That was exhausting," West says as a nurse reappears to connect him back to his machines.

"I know." I sit on the edge of his bed once the nurse is finished. "What do you want to do with the rest of the night?"

"I want to forget about everything and just watch a couple of really shitty horror movies."

I laugh and swing my legs into the bed beside him, leaning back against the pillows.

"I think we can manage that."

West nestles himself into my side as I scroll through the television channels, looking for a horror movie. I'm in the same frame of mind that he is. I don't want to think about being cut open in a matter of days and having part of my liver removed. I don't want to think about how much it's going to hurt or how long the healing is going to take.

And I don't want to dwell on the fact that when I'd confessed my feelings to him, he didn't say the words back to me. My heart ached that night, and I feel a dull pain even now. West may never love me, and I'll have to accept it. But right now, my first priority is to do whatever it takes to get him better.

There's no time to be scared or worried about what's going to happen to me. West is already scared enough for the both of us.

Instead of worrying about what comes next, I focus on the moment, enjoying having West wrapped in my arms. We don't need to worry about tomorrow because we have tonight to pretend everything is alright.

Chapter 24

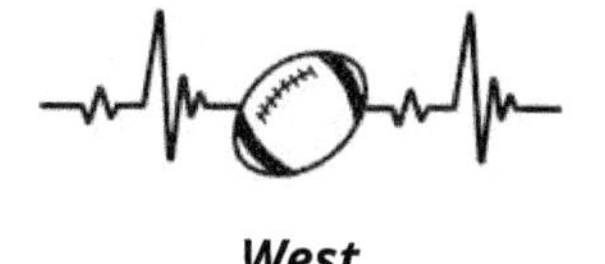

West

Two days pass in a blur of paperwork and bloodwork. There's barely an hour that goes by where I'm not panicking about what is about to happen. I've never had any big surgeries like this and at night I dream of never coming off the operating table.

Shane likes to tell me I'm being morbid when I wake up in the middle of the night covered in sweat and screaming. He's the one that sits beside me until I'm calm again and holds me until I'm asleep.

If it weren't for him, I don't think I would have made it this far.

When he comes to my room the morning of the surgery, Mom doesn't say anything but gives him a polite smile and a hug before leaving. It's an improvement over how she was treating him.

"Hey," Shane says as he stops beside my bed and looks down at me. "You look like shit."

"You don't look much better." I grin up at him. My body feels worse than ever, but for once my mind isn't running through all the different ways I could die in the span of the next few hours.

"I'm hot and you know it." He says with a smirk as he sits on the edge of my bed. "How's your head this morning?"

"For the first time in weeks, I finally feel like there's something to keep me going. I have a new chance at life, you know? I don't want to head into it thinking the worst is going to happen."

"That's probably a good way to look at it," Shane says, running his hand through his hair. "I'm honestly terrified of what could happen. I keep sitting back and thinking about it, worrying that something could go wrong."

"They're good doctors and Dr. Sullivan says that the specialist she's brought in for the transplant is one of the best in the country. There's nothing to worry about."

"Look at us, our roles have reversed." Shane smiles. "You used to be so pessimistic about all of this."

I take his hand and lace my fingers through his. I kiss the back of his hand, tears starting to blur my vision as I look up at him. "You've given me this chance at life. I couldn't ask for anything else."

Shane leans down and kisses me softly, his fingers running through my hair before he cups my jaw. I don't think I'll ever get tired of kissing him. His lips are soft and slow against mine. When he pulls away, I feel his absence like a dull ache.

"I wish we could do more right now," I say, my cheeks warming. "I imagine your first semester of college has been pretty boring compared to some of your friends. I know when I was your age, I was running around with a new girl every week. I feel bad for chaining you to me like this."

Shane pins me with his intense gaze. "I'm going to say this once, Weston Perkins, the fucking Third, so you better listen good. I wouldn't be here if I didn't want to be. I made a choice a long time ago to be by your side through this, and I don't give a shit about what this semester has been like. All I care about is you."

I don't know what to say to that. My heart and face warm significantly as I stare at him, wondering how I got lucky enough to have a man like him walk into my life. He's the best friend I've had in a long time.

Instead of trying to find the words I don't know how to say, I kiss him again.

Our kiss ends when my mom clears her throat. A nurse stands beside her, holding a clipboard and looking at Shane. My cheeks are considerably hotter as Shane pulls back.

"I'll see you after surgery," he says before following the nurse out of the room.

Mom enters the room with her cup of coffee. The dark circles beneath her eyes are finally starting to fade, though the new wrinkles and grey hairs are there to stay. She smiles at me before taking a seat on the edge of my bed.

For a few moments, she says nothing, just sips on her coffee and watches me. I start to squirm under her stare, wondering what she thinks of what she just saw. I want to talk to her about it, but I have no clue how. Even though we started to talk about it last week, I'm still worried. She could have changed her mind or decided she still doesn't like Shane.

"You look like I'm the monster that's going to drag you under the bed." Her smile grows as she takes another sip of her coffee. "Calm down. I've seen two men kiss before and I already figured out the two of you are dating."

"We're not dating." I sound unsure even to myself. "I don't know what we are. He's a guy I met at school that I really like, and I don't know what to do with that information."

"Why not? You told me you're bisexual and I would say you two feel pretty deeply for each other."

"What's everyone on the team going to think when I come back to school with a boyfriend?"

"Why do you care what they think?" She sets her coffee to the side. "The way I see it, if they're really your friends, they're going to support you no matter who you're dating. If they stop talking to you because that just so happens to be Shane, then that's their problem."

"I didn't expect you to be so calm and understanding about this." I regret the words the moment I see the hurt look cross her face.

"I know I haven't always been the most understanding mother. You've always been so different from the rest of the family, and I've never been sure how to interact with you. I've tried to love you the best way I know how, but I know at times it's harsh and overbearing."

"You're a good mom. We've just never connected the way you have with Thomas and Laurie."

Her eyes shine as she takes my hand and squeezes it. "I connect with them more because I can relate to them better and that's no excuse. I should have been at all of your games and shown you I will be behind you no matter what. Instead, I've let you think that it's easier to go through a difficult diagnosis and potential death on your own. I never want to make you feel like that again, Weston."

I sniffle and wipe away a tear. "I wanted you to be at those games, Mom. I wanted to feel like you wanted to see me play, but you were never there for me the way you were for Thomas and Laurie."

Tears roll down her cheeks as she nods. "I know, honey. I'm not going to let you feel that way again. I'm going to be there for every game. Every big moment in your life, your dad and I will be there."

"You really will?"

"Really, Weston," Dad says as he walks into the room and pulls me into a tight hug. Laurie and Thomas are close behind him. “We’re going to make this family feel more like a family.”

There is a knock on the door, breaking us apart, as a team of nurses enters. The one in the middle smiles and steps into the room.

“I hate to break this up, but it’s time that we take Weston for surgery now.”

“I love you.” Mom kisses my forehead. “I’ll see you after the surgery is over and for what it’s worth, I really like your boyfriend. He seems like the kind of man you need in your life. He balances you out well.”

“I love you too, Mom,” I say, the lump in my throat nearly choking me.

After I say my goodbyes to the rest of my family, the nurses prep me for surgery. I try not to focus on what is about to happen, instead looking forward to seeing Shane after all this is over. I don’t know what I’m going to say to him, but I know I want to be with him for as long as he’ll have me.

Knowing I’m on the borderline of living and dying, I don’t want to waste any more time pretending to be someone I’m not.

Shane’s been there with me through it all. He’s held my hand at my lowest of lows and he’s given me a chance to live again.

I don’t care what my teammates are going to think. When I go back to school, I want to have Shane by my side for that, too. I want my friends to know how I feel about him and all he has done for me.

I don't want to spend one more moment pretending he hasn't turned my entire life around.

As the anesthesiologist fits the mask over my face, instructing me to count down from one hundred, my thoughts are on Shane.

CHAPTER 25

Shane

I've never been in more pain in my life. My stomach feels like it's trying to fight its way free from my body, even with all the medication they're pumping into me. I knew the surgery would be painful, but I didn't think it would be this bad.

It doesn't matter though. I would do it all over again for West. Hell, if he asked for a piece of every other organ in my body, I would gladly give it.

The nurses wheeled him in a few hours ago, but he hasn't woken up yet. His soft snores fill the room, and I wonder if his pain compares to mine. I imagine it would after he's been cut open and had his organs rearranged.

When he finally wakes up, I'm watching a horror movie and trying to forget the amount of pain I'm in. I consider calling the nurse and asking for more drugs, but I don't think it would do any good.

"You're awake," West says as he turns his head to the side and looks at me. "I didn't know if you would be awake yet or not."

"I've been awake for a couple of hours. They started my surgery before yours, remember?"

West chuckles and shakes his head. "All I remember is the gas man giving me gas and then the world went hazy."

I laugh and roll my eyes. "You're still buzzed, baby. Why don't you just sit back and watch the movie until your head is a little clearer?"

"You should be on this level," West says, holding his hand up in front of him and wiggling his fingers. "It's a good level. I think that everyone should be on this level."

I turn off the movie and close my eyes. "Maybe we should just go to sleep instead. We have a video call with the university in the morning and I doubt you being high is going to help with that."

"I hope I can still finish my course load this year," West says, his voice sounding soft and dreamy. I keep my eyes closed, hoping he'll do the same. "And then we have to tell them why you've been a shit student all semester."

I chuckle. "Thanks, West. Now go to sleep."

"Night, Shane."

"Night, West."

***

When we wake in the morning, my head is still spinning and the pain feels worse. I know it's going to hurt for a while, but that doesn't mean I'm not wishing the pain would go away now.

I call Uncle James before West's mom brings in a laptop. He doesn't say much on the call, other than he'll be in to visit me sometime this afternoon.

I'm not sure if that's a good thing or a bad thing.

He offered to be here yesterday, but I turned him down. I didn't want him here. I wanted my mom, but I couldn't have her, and Uncle James was no replacement. Being with West was enough.

Now, I wasn't so sure. Seeing West interact with his family, I want my own family around, even if that family is just Uncle James.

"How are you doing?" West asks as he looks over at me, adjusting the angle of his bed slightly so he's in a more upright position for the video call.

"I feel like shit but it was worth it."

Some of the color is returning to West's cheeks and there's a spark in his eyes that I haven't seen in a while. It's good to see him looking healthier than he has in a long time. I want to climb into his bed with him and watch more movies, but there are other matters we have to deal with.

West's mom sticks around long enough to connect the video call for us before leaving. She shuts the door behind her and then it is just West and me alone with the disciplinary committee.

"Good morning, ladies and gentlemen," Uncle James says as he takes his seat at the head of the table. "We've come here today to discuss the matter of Shane Johnson. Since Shane is in the hospital at the moment, this meeting must be conducted remotely."

"Thank you," I say, swallowing hard and trying not to think about the sweat beading on my forehead. "I know that my absence from lectures and classes has been significant over the last semester. I also know this school has given me a chance to prove myself beyond the alleged forged test scores."

"Yes, and in that time, you have done nothing but make a mockery of the offer extended to you," one of the professors says as she leans forward in her seat to look through a document in front of her. "It would appear you've missed more time than you have been present for, especially in recent weeks."

"That would be my fault," West says, waving to the committee. "I was diagnosed with juvenile hemochromatosis not that long ago and with that came liver failure. During these last few weeks, I've been hospitalized and Shane has been with me, keeping me company and in the end, he has donated a portion of his liver. Without him, I would be dead."

Some of the professors start whispering amongst themselves and I feel a small ray of hope rising in my chest. I think this may go better than I originally thought. Uncle James passes out a document I sent him. A few nights ago, West and I sat down and compared the days

I missed school to the days I was with him, taking him to clinics and sitting with him until he was alright.

The professors say nothing as they sort through the documents, their eyebrows furrowing. They flip over the page, moving on to the next one. It's a few minutes before they finally clear their throats and look up.

"Well, it seems that there has been a lot of activity in your life and while we commend you for supporting a friend in need, we cannot condone this kind of action, especially when our reputation as a university is on the line," the professor says, pushing the papers to the side. "I move for immediate expulsion."

"His absence without informing anyone is my fault," West says, speaking up before someone has a chance to say anything else. "I asked him not to tell anyone what was happening in my private life. Shane was kind enough to respect that, knowing it would result in potential problems for him."

"I move that Shane be allowed to continue his study upon his recovery from surgery," a different professor says. "He has shown a great amount of character in supporting his friend. We wish to send students out into the world who are well-rounded and the best representation of Tennessee University. I believe Shane is one of those upstanding students. Even in his absence from class, his grades have not deteriorated."

"I second that motion." Uncle James looks around the room. "We shall take a vote."

I hold my breath as they disappear into another room to vote. I can feel West's eyes on me, but I can't bring myself to look at him. This moment is too big. Too important. This is the moment that decides the rest of my life.

When the professors return to the video call, Uncle James is smiling. I feel the hope soar in my chest as the other professors shake his hand before leaving the room.

"While you've been absent," Uncle James says the moment the professors are gone. "We can all agree it was for a good cause. As far as the university is concerned, you are welcome to return and finish your studies. As well, we will be recommending you to any other university, provided you finish out your second semester strong."

"Thank you," I say, finally feeling the weight that has been sitting on my chest lifted. "I'll see you later?"

"I'll be there in a few hours."

He ends the call, and I turn to West with a broad smile. Everything is going to be alright. West has a new liver and I get to pursue as much education as I want without worrying about the allegedly forged test scores.

"Congratulations," West says as he shifts slightly to reach across the gap between our beds.

I shift and reach for him, our fingers lacing together. I stare at him for a moment, wondering what comes next for us. Though I want to keep seeing him, I know this has only been an experiment in sexuality for him. Even if it does feel like both of us have growing feelings for each other.

Still, I don't know if the threat of death disappearing changes anything for us.

I swallow hard and let go of his hand to run my hand through my hair. "What happens with us now?"

"What do you mean?" West asks, a line appearing between his eyebrows. "What do you want to happen between us?"

"I already told you; I'm not going to push you into anything you don't want to do. I have thoughts on what I would like to see happen between us, but they're only thoughts."

"If I told you I'm in love with you and want to try dating you for real, would that scare you away?" West asks, his gaze locking with mine.

"Not even a little," I say, reaching across the gap to hold his hand again.

***

Uncle James walks into the room with a bag of movies. He grins as he sets the bag on the couch in the corner before walking over to me. To my surprise, he leans over the bed and pulls me into a tight hug. I hear him sniff as he pulls back and see his red-rimmed eyes up close for the first time.

"Your mom would be so proud of you, Shane," he says as he sits on the edge of my bed. He looks over at West. "Well?"

"Uncle James, this is my boyfriend, Weston Perkins," I say, smiling so hard it hurts. It's the first time I've been able to introduce West as my boyfriend and it feels good.

Epilogue

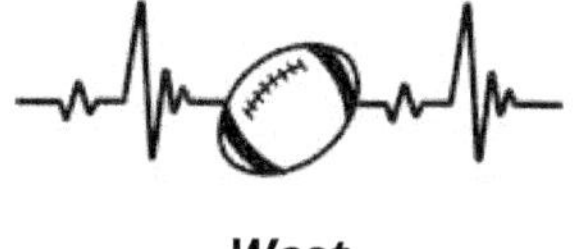

West

One Year Later

Nobody tells you about all the things that can change in the span of a year. Shane and I are about to finish our fourth year of college. Graduation is only a few weeks away. We fought and laughed and cried more than I ever have in my life.

Every moment spent with him makes me feel more alive than the last.

If you had told me a little over a year ago that I would be here, madly in love with the man I know is the love of my life, I would say you were crazy.

Now, as I sit on the couch holding his hand, I can't believe where my life has taken me.

Getting sick is the worst thing that's ever happened to me, but in a way, it's also the best. It brought me closer to my family, and without my diagnosis, Shane would have never come crashing into my life and claimed his place there.

"Are you ready to go?" Mom sweeps into the room, adjusting her hair before smoothing out her gown. "They've got our table ready and they're about to start announcing the first-round picks soon."

I take a deep breath and stand up, pulling Shane up with me. There's a soft smile on his face as he reaches out to adjust my tie. Shane's hands run down the front of my suit jacket, smoothing out the wrinkles and making me look presentable.

"You look amazing," he says as he adjusts my tie again, his grin widening as he pats my chest. "Can you believe we're here right now? It seems surreal. You worked so hard for all of this."

"I didn't think this day would ever come," I whisper back, running a hand through my hair. Shane swats my hand away and quickly fixes whatever I messed up. "Thank you for everything."

"Don't thank me," he says. "I do it because I love you."

He kisses me lightly before leading the way out of the room. We walk down the long hall before entering the ballroom where the draft is being held. An usher greets us and directs us to our table. Mom takes her seat with Dad on one side of her and my siblings on the other.

Shane and I take our seats as the rest of the attendees shuffle into the room and take theirs.

"You look nervous," Shane whispers as he leans closer to me. "Smile. This is going to be the best day of your life."

"I'm nervous," I whisper back, squeezing his hand tighter. "What if I don't make it? What if I'm not good enough?"

"You worked your ass off to recover and get back in the game. You earned this. They're going to call you and you're going to the NFL, baby. Stop doubting yourself."

I let his words sink in.

The evening is a blur, as there are probably dozens of speeches that have to be rendered before they start announcing the drafts. When the NFL commissioner walks onto the stage to announce the teams, it seems like the entire room is holding their breath.

I know several scouts have had their eyes on me, but whether they put my name down in the draft or not, I have no way of knowing.

"The Miami Sabres have selected Weston Perkins," the commissioner says, his voice booming through the sound system.

My family screams and claps, cheering as Shane urges me to my feet. I walk across the room to where the Sabres' general manager is waiting. He grins as we shake hands.

"Welcome to the team, Perkins. We've been looking for a tight end with your abilities."

"Thank you for the opportunity."

As I walk back to my table, my heart is hammering in my chest. All of this feels like a fever dream. It's time to pack up and move to a new state.

I'm going to be in the NFL. I get to play football for a living and have a college education under my belt. None of it feels real. A year ago, I thought I was going to die, and now I'm sitting like I'm on top of the world. I've gotten everything I've ever wanted in life.

Nothing can beat the way I feel now.

Except maybe the way I feel when Shane tells me he loves me.

As I sit down beside him, I wonder what he's thinking. We've only ever talked about moving together in the abstract. It was always if I got into the NFL then we could move to one place or the other together, but we've never made an actual decision.

All I know is that I love him too much to lose him.

There are only about a dozen or so queer players in the NFL, and I've made no secret of the fact that I'm an out player.

"Miami," Shane whispers, leaning closer to me. "How are you feeling? This is exciting. I'm proud of you."

"What are we going to do?"

"Well," Shane says, a sly smile crossing his face. "I may have begged Coach Veer for some confidential information a few months ago on which states were considering you seriously. And then I might have applied to all of those schools that are nearby, seeing if I could get into a graduate school wherever you lived."

"And?" I ask, holding my breath and crossing my fingers. I want him to move with me, but I won't ask him to give up his future to be with me.

"I got into Miami U."

"We're *both* moving to Miami?" I ask, not quite believing what he's telling me. "You're shitting me. You applied to Miami U, and you got in?"

"I got in."

"I can't believe you did that without telling me."

Shane smiles, reaching out to cup my jaw. I lean into his touch, completely lost in how much I love him.

"Why would you do that?" My voice is nearly a whisper as my family celebrates around us.

"A long time ago, I decided I was willing to do whatever it takes to love you for the rest of my life."

Extended Epilogue

Shane

Three Years Later

Graduate school has been kicking my ass. After graduating from TU with my bachelor's and moving from Tennessee, I'd opted to defer my studies at Miami U, so both West and I could settle, and I could attend as many of his away games as possible to support him. Then months later, I started my graduate studies. The first year wasn't so bad, but my second year is hell. Working towards a Master's Degree in Economics is draining my energy every single day, but it's worth it when I consider how proud my mom would be.

Graduate school wouldn't have even been possible if Uncle James and the disciplinary team hadn't made calls to the college board after my first semester at TU.

From what Uncle James told me, there had been two different Shanes taking their SATs in the same testing center at the same time. While my scores were accurate and not forged, the other Shane had forged his scores. The college board messed up our last names, switching them on the paperwork and making it appear as if I had forged my scores.

After the college board admitted to their mistake, my record was wiped clean, and I was free to pursue my education the way I had always dreamed of.

It might not have been Yale or Dartmouth, but TU and the college board's mistake brought me to West.

West is away at a game while I'm at home with my nose buried in case studies and various reports. He's been thriving in the NFL. I've been at as many games as I can, but it's difficult when I have school to attend in Miami.

"I'm home!" West shouts as the front door opens and slams behind him. We bought a house together after West got another signing bonus when he signed a five-year contract with Miami.

I get up from my desk and meet him in the hallway, wrapping him in a hug and kissing him. I hate the time we have to spend away from each other, but coming back together feels that much better.

"You ready to head to the airport?" He grabs the suitcase I put by the door earlier that morning.

"As ready as I'll ever be." I pull on my sneakers before heading back into the living room and stuffing my books into my bag.

We are going back to Tennessee for a week to spend some time with his sister and our new niece. She was born a couple weeks ago, but this is the first chance we've had to go see her.

Once I gather my textbooks and laptop, we head out the door and make the drive to the airport, talking about how West's game went.

***

Instead of driving toward Laurie's house after we arrive in Tennessee, West takes a different road that leads us to the waterfall where I took him camping four years ago.

"What are we doing?" I ask as he turns onto a dirt road.

"I had Thomas come up here and set a tent up for us. I thought we could have a little alone time together after I got back from my trip before we launched into a week of non-stop family activities."

I grin and reach out to lace my fingers through his as he pulls into the same campsite I brought him to years ago. The waterfall still stands tall as it crashes down into the lake below. There's a new wooden railing that circles the campsite, keeping people from stumbling over the edge of the cliff. The red picnic table was now yellow and the fire pit had been expanded. A small charcoal barbecue stands off to the side.

Unlike the last time we were up here, there are lights strung between the trees and soft music playing in the background. Thomas had thought of everything when he came here and set up our camp.

There is a part of me that can't believe West put this much thought into a night away together. There is another part that isn't surprised at all. Since we became a couple, there hasn't been a day that goes by where he hasn't made me feel like the most important person in his life.

I start to tear up as we get out of the rental truck. When we moved to Miami, I wasn't sure I would ever come back here again. It felt wrong to leave the waterfall behind after spending so many trips with my mom here and then bringing West. It was the place where I first knew without a doubt that I loved him.

As I turn around to face West, my heart catches in my throat. He's down on one knee with a black velvet box open in his hand. A silver band is nestled inside the fabric and there's a smile on his face.

"Shane, I fell in love with you before you ever decided mutilation seemed like a good way to be my friend," he says, joking about his transplant. Over the years, it has been a running joke between us. I liked to say it was the only way I could get his attention and prove that I'd truly love him.

"Are you really doing this right now?" I grin so hard it hurts as my heart hammers in my chest.

"Shane, I'm going to love you until the day I die and then so many more years after that. Will you marry me?"

"Yes!"

I kneel in front of him and kiss him, my fingers weaving through his hair as his arms wrap around me. When he pulls back, there's a smile on his face.

"Give me your hand." He takes the ring out of the box. I hold my hand out to him and he slips the ring over my finger. "I love you."

"I love you too."

I stand up and take his hand, pulling him with me. He follows me into the tent and our clothes hit the ground.

West drops to his knees, fisting my cock with one hand as he licks the head. He trails a line with his tongue, following the vein of my cock before he opens his mouth wider and takes me in.

"Fuck yes," I groan as he toys with my balls while sucking hard. My hips rock in time with his sucking as my eyes close and my head falls back.

"Not yet." West pulls back from me with an impish smile. "I want you to fuck me."

We move to the air mattress that's already set up. West moans as I trail kisses down his body until his cock is in my mouth. He's thrusting his hips in time with my sucking as I circle my finger around his hole.

West moves slightly, and there's the sound of something unzipping before a bottle of lube lands beside me. I chuckle around his cock before taking him deeper and sucking harder. He shivers as the cold lube makes contact with his skin, moaning as I push a finger inside him. I thrust slowly, giving him time to get accustomed to the single finger before I add another.

"Flip over," I say, waiting as he moves before pushing two fingers inside him again and wrapping my other hand around his hard length.

My thumb brushes over the head of his cock as I add a third finger. I swirl the salty drop around the head, massaging it in before stroking his cock hard, in time with the thrusts of my fingers. West jerks in my hand, his cock straining as his moans echo around us.

"Tell me, Shane."

"'In case you ever foolishly forget; I'm never not thinking of you.' That's Virginia Woolf, baby." I lower my head and kiss him softly. "I'm always, *always* thinking of you."

I pull back and sit back on my heels, squirting more lube onto him, working it in before lining up my cock with his entrance. West groans as I thrust into him, sinking myself as deep as I can before pulling out and slamming into him again. He moans and reaches for his cock, stroking himself frantically.

We fall over the edge together before collapsing into a tangle of limbs on the mattress. West rolls over and nestles himself into my side, leaning over quickly to bite my nipple before laughing.

"You're such a little shit." Amidst his teasing laughter, I rise to my feet and start searching through a backpack his brother must have put in the tent for something to clean up with.

Once we're cleaned up, I lay down beside him and wrap my arms around him. West sighs and leans into me, his eyes closing.

"I love you," I say as I kiss his temple. "I can't believe we're going to get married."

West chuckles. "Believe it, sweetheart. There's no one I'd rather spend the rest of my life with than you...only you. I'm always thinking of you and there isn't a single world where I could ever exist without you."

We lose ourselves in each other again, loving each other more than we ever have. As we snuggle together, talking about our dream wedding, I can't wait to tell all our friends and family.

While he snores softly, curled into my embrace, I'm convinced there's no world in which I could ever live without him either.

I press my lips to his forehead in the softest of kisses...and sigh. This beautiful man came into my life at a time when I was at my lowest, a piece of me was missing. But every single day, he lifts me up and fills my empty spaces.

A long time ago, West told me I'm his savior because I literally saved his life; but the way I see it, we saved each other.

The End

AFTERWORD

Thank you for taking a chance on *SAVING WEST* and trusting me to give you a few hours of reading pleasure. I'd be happy if you could do me one favor. Many potential readers depend on honest reviews to determine if they should One-Click a book. Please help them make an informed decision by posting a review of *SAVING WEST*. Your review doesn't have to be long.

I love hearing from readers, so you may shoot me an email at denvershawromance@gmail.com. That's how our friendship will begin, if we aren't friends already. You may also send me a friend request on Facebook or join my Facebook group @devonshawromance. Don't forget to follow me on TikTok and Instagram @devonshawromance.

I also hope you'll consider joining my mailing list. By doing this, you'll receive updates on my upcoming releases, giveaways, deals, and free reads. It will surely be an honor if you decide to subscribe. To join my mailing list, visit devonshawromance.com

Kind regards, always,
Denver

Acknowledgments

Without the time, patience, and effort of two lovely ladies, launching my debut MM romance novel would not have been possible. Thus, it would be remiss of me to not express my eternal gratitude for their contribution and give them the recognition they rightly deserve.

Kari Monty came into my life like the breath of fresh air that she is. She designed my logo and covers for the three books in the Tennessee U series, as well as created my website, newsletter, graphics, social media, and so much more.

Angela O'Connell worked diligently on making Shane and West's story shine. Changing words for variation, deleting things that were repetitive, switching words from British to American English, and making sure I used the present tense consistently were just some of what Angela did to make Saving West better than it was when I submitted it to her for editing.

By doing all these things, Kari and Angela gave me the time I needed to finish Shane and West's story. They truly embody the spirit of Indie Author Creative, which was established so that every author who is under their care, can go write because they've got the rest.

Thank you, thank you, thank you, for all you've done.

About Author

Denver Shaw is a girl who enjoys the simple things in life: the first sip of coffee in the morning, the changing colors of sunset, and clothes fresh out of the dryer- although she doesn't enjoy folding them. When she isn't reading romance stories, she spends her time plotting and writing them.

To find out more about Denver, follow her on:

Instagram @denvershawromance

TikTok @denvershawromance

Subscribe to her newsletter at denvershawromance.com or send her an email at denvershawromance@gmail.com.

Lightning Source UK Ltd.
Milton Keynes UK
UKHW021850090223
416682UK00014B/1601